VIOLET HONEY

HARET CHRONICLES QILIN: SUGAR BITES TWO

LAUREL CHASE

DEDICATION

This series is for all the girls who like sex and sugar.

So, that's everyone, right?

Carry on.

CHAPTER ONE

CARLYLE

Toro was trying to play it cool as he sauntered into my bedroom, but I could tell my fish was gasping for air on the inside. He gave me a huge grin, and through the water magic we shared, I felt how every cell in his body was practically vibrating.

"What is it, keeper?" I asked, standing and wrapping my arms around his trim waist.

He dropped a chaste kiss on the tip of my nose, even as his palms cupped under my ass cheeks. I snickered. Always full of contradictions, my ocean man.

"I found the coolest fucking thing," he said, bouncing on the balls of his feet and rubbing our bodies against each other. I couldn't quite decide if it was adorable or fucking hot. Either way, I couldn't quit smiling back at him.

"Are you gonna tell me or just tease?" I prompted. He shrugged, and I laughed. I knew whatever it was would come spilling out soon enough. Toro was a tease, but he had a big mouth, too.

"I found something in the pool we're building!" he gloated, proving my theory.

"And?" I hadn't been down to that level of our new castle home in nearly a week.

After chasing that fucking leprechaun all around Haret and Earth, I'd sort of taken a break from any exploring - from pretty much anything, actually. Instead, I'd been lounging in my bed and gorging on whatever sweets my men brought me - including every flavor of mate I had.

"There's water, *under the water*!" Toro said, taking a huge step away and dragging me along. I tripped over my feet trying to hurry after him, finally grabbing the chance to hop onto his back as he started down the stone stairs.

"What does 'water under the water' mean, exactly?" I asked, wrapping my arms around his neck and my legs around his waist. He bounded down the two levels to the basement area while I sucked on his neck and pretended to be an octopus stuck to his back.

We'd decided the lowest level was the perfect spot to convert into an indoor pool for Toro to keep comfortable in, and my shifters had jumped right into the remodeling vibe. Really, it was turning out to be more of a grotto, and I was in love with the whole mermaid vibe.

"Look!" he said, hauling me around in his arms and pointing to the far edge of the pool. "See that darkness down there? We broke through some more stone to make the pool deeper and found a natural spring. It's fucking deep, too. There's an aquifer down there, baby!"

I smiled at him, still not one hundred percent sure why this was so exciting. But Toro was happy, and that made me happy.

"You need to come exploring with me," he continued, setting me on my feet. I could already feel his mer magic pulsing and reaching for me. It had been weeks since he'd used his siren song and lure magic to shift me into a mer, and at the suggestion, I was definitely sharing the excitement.

"Hold on, mer. She's not going anywhere," Jai barked, striding in from the room I'd begun referring to as the dungeon. Thank the goddess, there weren't any real cells down here, but it was still creepy as fuck. None of us had any idea how old the castle truly was, or who else had lived in it besides Iaga and her mates, over a century ago.

"I can keep her safe," Toro said, bristling. His

chest puffed up behind me, and I sent Jai a look, mentally warning him to back his overprotective self off.

The stubborn-ass vampire only held my eyes with a blank look and gave a tiny shake of his head.

His voice echoed in my mind, flat and uncompromising. *It's unexplored territory - and that's too dangerous. Especially right now.*

I wanted to backtalk - to insist he was babying me - but honestly, I'd sort of lost my nerve after the leprechaun's weird rhymes concerning the first-born child I didn't have.

The first-born I had no way of having, unless I took a Qilin mate. That thought squirmed all over me, and I snuggled up to Toro.

"You check it out first, fish," I said, reaching up to plant a kiss on his full lips. "I promise I'll come see it soon." The pleading look I was giving him did the trick, and he melted against me.

"Of course, baby. I just got excited, is all."

I could tell by his tone that he'd instantly forgiven and forgotten, but his words ripped at my heart a little. I wanted to live, damn it. I didn't want to hole up in a stone fortress, afraid of every little thing that might happen.

I still had a huge bucket list of places I wanted to see, both in Haret and back on Earth. If I couldn't get excited about living a full life with my men, then what was even the point?

The point is to keep you alive long enough to stabilize

Haret, Jai hissed in my mind. I bit down on a sigh - sneaky fucking vampire had been skimming my thoughts again.

Something which shouldn't be so easy. Build your mental walls stronger, Carlyle, or I'll-

You'll what? I challenged him back, sending my thought slamming into his brain. *I seem to remember liking the ways you taught me to build my walls*, I taunted, my body rubbing against Toro while I flashed Jai images of him breaking my mind while he worshiped my body.

What I wouldn't have given for him to just go with the moment now. But he huffed and turned on his heel, his steps silent on the stone floors. I glared after him for a second before deciding I didn't have to be scared of *everything*.

"Maybe just a dip in the shallow end? How's the water, fish?" I murmured against Toro's lips, willing myself to forget about Jai's fears and the stupid threats of danger we thought we'd left behind after stabilizing the Path.

"A little chilly, but I can warm you up just fine," my mer said, tipping us straight over the edge of the pool before I could gather a full breath.

We surfaced together, and he pressed me against the stone ledge, smothering me in kisses. I reveled in the feeling while his hands worked to free my body from its soggy clothing. The contrast of the cool water and the heat of his skin on mine was amazing, and I tilted my head back onto the ledge as he kissed and nipped down my neck.

His muscled chest pinned me to the rough wall of the pool, and I slid my hand down the smooth planes of his back, fingertips skittering over his newly shifted tail. The flutter of his tail fin crept between my calves, then drifted up the backs of my thighs.

"Sing for me, mer," I whispered, and his gorgeous siren song began to pull me under its hypnotic spell.

Soon enough, I was completely lost in my mer's ocean of pleasure, chasing the oblivion I craved.

No matter how hard I chased, though, something else was quick to follow in my mind. Darkness hovered in the depths of my thoughts, just like the darkness that swirled in the far bottom corner of the pool.

We'd saved Haret, and each day brought new fun, but something wasn't quite right yet.

CHAPTER TWO

JAI

I paced my way back into the dungeon - so aptly named for the amount of time I'd spent down here. Carlyle had even begun cracking jokes about me being the crypt keeper, which were a little funnier to her than me.

All I wanted to do was take my *aima* to Paris on a later-than-late honeymoon. Yet here we were, solving more goddamn riddles and trying to keep our Queen safe without tipping her off about the depth of the danger.

I hadn't even had a spare moment to check on the state of Saori Sang and the mess my mother was still creating there. I didn't even know if Kana had slunk back in there yet, or if she'd taken my advice and gone to stay with Grand-Mère first.

Dair eyed me as I entered the stone room. Torches ringed the space, casting more than enough light to read by. Of course, the castle had a proper library, but neither of us wanted Carlyle to stumble on the sort of books we'd been using to research the odd green stone left by the leprechaun.

"She's going to figure us out," Dair muttered, repeating his warning for the millionth fucking time. I didn't even bother to tamp down the growl rumbling in my throat.

"I don't fucking care, mage. I care more about keeping her safe than mollifying her."

He raised an eyebrow at me, smirking. Yeah, I knew it was at least half a goddamn lie. There was no winning in that choice. Either Carlyle was safe and pissed, or she was in danger.

I started to open my mouth to rail at him instead of the situation when the distinct popping noise of a mage siphoning reached my sensitive ears.

"What is it?" Dair called as I bolted from the room. Streaking into the pool area, I paused to appreciate Carlyle and Toro tangled together in the water. Her white-blond hair was spread out on the surface of the dark water, and her eyes were dilated in pleasure when she glanced up at me.

I nearly forgot why I'd bolted in here.

"*Jai?*" Dair called in my mind, and I ripped my

eyes from Carlyle's. No - it hadn't been her siphoning.

Then who?

I answered him, *Get upstairs. Someone's siphoned into the castle.*

He and I arrived in the main foyer at nearly the same moment, his body popping into view right in front of our mystery guest.

"Well, fuck," I muttered as Dair gave a forced grin and stepped forward to embrace his mother. I waved away the shifter guards who had just rushed into the room.

We'd fortified the castle several times against many sorts of intrusions, but it seemed there were still a few fucking holes in our defense.

"Tilda," I said, nodding briskly to her. I ignored her Council title of Second Chairperson just to push her buttons. "What business are you on?"

Barely listening to her nonsense answer, I sent rapid-fire instructions to Killian to round up the handful of mages we had on staff. We needed to check the perimeter for magical breaches again - the property was just so fucking huge.

"Such dreadful hospitality, Alisdair. Not to mention, quite a lack of security," Tilda chided, her shrill voice breaking into my mental tirade. Guess she wasn't above pushing buttons, either.

Her eyes slid past me as though I were nothing more than furniture. Dair's mother could be useful, but there was no love lost between us. She'd always believed Dair was destined to lead our team instead of me, and when he'd announced his mating to Carlyle instead of another well-bred mage, she'd been less than impressed with that, too.

Her only son rejecting his coveted Council seat had been the last straw for her, placing every one of us in unfavorable places on her exceptionally long shit list.

"Why are you here, exactly, Mother?" Dair asked again.

She sighed and placed her hands on her hips. "As you suspect, I'm not here on a pleasure visit. The Council has news of continued and growing restlessness and even a few minor scuffles between groups in the outlying communities. It's centered mainly around the darkblood groups. We've brought a few in for questioning, and they all seem to think our new Queen of Haret has ideas to eradicate certain *types* of Haretians. Again - darkblood types. Might you two know where that rumor began?"

Dair and I exchanged a glance that Tilda didn't miss. She narrowed her eyes at us the way only a powerful woman can - but unfortunately for her, we were well-acquainted with a woman like that. I wasn't immune to Carlyle's challenge stares, but anyone else's had certainly lost effect.

Dair stepped forward and grasped her elbow lightly. "I have a story to tell you, Mother. Shall we go somewhere more comfortable? I'll call for someone to make us some fresh tea and bring those little shifter cakes you enjoy." His voice was conciliatory, and she sniffed, knowing she was being placated.

She followed him, though, glaring back at me as they left the room, heading in the direction of the regular library.

I tossed out a mental order for the rest of the team to gather in the throne room. We had lots to discuss, and if the rumors of darkblood rebellions had already reached Patriam, we needed to move fast.

DAIR

"I want to go see Dr. F in Aralia," Carlyle announced, and the room settled into silence. "He's the only one I trust to help me figure out this firstborn thing."

"What's to figure out?" Mother asked dryly. She had been less than impressed with my recitation of the leprechaun's false curse and following death, or his haunting riddle about a future child, the balance tilting, and even more fucking secrets.

Per Jai's instruction, I'd carefully left out the bit about the heartstone we'd found hiding beneath the glamor of the leprechaun's gold. Even Carlyle hadn't been told about that mystery, and the stone was currently sitting in a glamored vault in the dungeon.

I could tell Mother thought she had all the answers, though. She was smirking and staring Carlyle down. "Qilin cannot mother children with non-Qilin. So unless you're planning yet *another* mating, there must be a different interpretation to that prophecy. Or perhaps it's all just rubbish spewed by a desperate fae." She glared in Killian's direction, and I nearly kicked her under the library table.

Just because racism was how she'd been raised didn't make it right, and I'd warned her more than once.

Toro jumped in though, his voice a touch louder than needed in the muted space. "There are other things to birth besides children. Like countries, laws, movements. Maybe the prophecy meant one of those."

"I am much less concerned about the meaning of this child-bearing prophecy than I am about the very real threats to our country," Mother snapped, and part of me knew she was right. We had two mysteries on our hands, and while I wasn't certain how they were linked, we couldn't simply ignore either one.

But my good girl had her eyes locked on the floor. I could tell she was breathing slow and deep in her belly, calming herself. Jai caught my eye and shook his head, agreeing with me. Our Queen was on the verge of a temper tantrum - and though perhaps rightly deserved - it was certainly something she would regret.

"Marcel is worth a shot," Killian muttered, surprising me. Of all of us, I'd expected his agreement least. After returning from Earth's Council, the fae doctor had settled back in Aralia, and Killian consistently wanted Carlyle as far from his homeland as possible.

"He's worth more than a shot," Carlyle said, standing stiffly. "It's the best fucking lead we have, since I shanked the leprechaun. Tilda, reassure the Council that his death was a result of self-defense, and I have no plans to eradicate anyone. But you guys managed not to have civil war before I got here, didn't you? Do your job a little longer, so I can figure out this riddle. It sounds like it might be worth the dark half of the kingdom."

She stalked from the room, Sol and Jack hurrying to follow her.

"Of course, we can handle the darkbloods," Mother said, glaring defensively after Carlyle.

"Of course, you can," I agreed. "Thank you very much for keeping us up to date. I promise we will do the same."

"She's speaking of that Council doctor known for his questionable methods, if I'm correct?" Mother asked, and I was relieved to hear the anger had left her voice. She smoothed back her hair, trying to hide the hint of a wrinkle between her brows. She acted contrary out of habit, but I knew deep down, she cared for Carlyle.

"Marcel may have done horrible things in his Council position, but Carlyle trusts him," Jai affirmed, his voice barely more than a growl. "And with her at least, he's proved himself honorable."

Toro shrugged. "If it makes our girl feel better to check it out, what harm can it be? We can all go and keep her safe. Aralia can't be as bad now that Ignea's gone."

Killian sighed, but he didn't contradict. "Let her have her way, or she'll jus' siphon there alone," he warned, rolling his eyes. We all knew he was right. "From what I hear, my brothers have kept fair order of the fae kingdom. I donna believe we'll be harmed there."

"Contact them, then," Jai ground out. "Arrange it."

"Shall I just siphon him there now?" I asked, keeping my voice light. After all, Carlyle would want to get this done quickly. Traditional methods of communication in Haret took days, and we'd all been a little spoiled by Earth's quickened pace.

Jai narrowed his eyes at me, but after a second, he nodded. "Arrange it," he repeated.

I caught just a hint of worry on Mother's face before Killian shrugged and linked elbows with me. I pulled us into the siphon, and we popped out the other side of the cosmos right at the virtual doorstep of Aralia.

A cadre of armed fae was upon us in seconds, but on recognizing Killian as one of their princes, they stood down easily. I couldn't help but grin - it was such a marked improvement since our previous visit, when the guards had mocked him for his disgraced status.

"Take us to the throne room and summon my siblings," Killian ordered, squaring his shoulders.

"And summon the doctor Marcel. We have some things to discuss in the name of the Qilin Queen."

I turned my face, hiding a different sort of smile now. It was excellent to see the fae take charge. He'd spent his entire life barely more than a slave to his mother.

Now he was mated to the Queen of all Haret, and he was finally getting comfortable with demanding the respect he'd been due all along.

Within minutes, we were seated in the height of fae luxury, being served drinks and hors d'oeuvres by beautiful, nearly naked fae servants.

Killian leaned into my shoulder. "I know they're still serving us, but they seem happier, right?"

I surveyed the fae milling about, gauging his observation. Nodding, I said, "Yes, I think they do. Your siblings may be better rulers than Ignea."

"They'll each have a cruel streak, for certain. But perhaps four in joint charge are better than a single one."

"Plus there is no need to fight over who has ultimate power," I added, pleased that he'd included himself among his brothers. Although he'd declined an active seat in Aralia when they asked, Killian was still considered an Aralian ruler. His brothers had been sending periodic reports of activity and decisions, though I doubted Kills had ever read any of them.

"Glad I've no true part in it, though," he muttered, as though hearing my thoughts. "I donna have the temper to rule. Rather spend my days with that sweet-tastin' Qilin anyway." He grinned, raising his eyebrows at me. "Jus' like you, eh, mage?"

"Absolutely," I said, my voice nearly a growl. My mother could keep the Council for herself. I had no desire to be in the middle of that mess again.

"Ya think Sol or Toro want any part o' their kingdoms?" he asked, a rare note of vulnerability creeping into his words.

"I don't, fae. Neither would Jai or Jack, if asked. We were all born to rule, yet I think supporting roles suit us better. Our Queen needs our power, and I'm quite willing to serve Haret in that manner."

Killian broke into raucous laughter. "Aye, giving her our power is the most fun I could imagine."

Our banter was ended by the echoes of soft footsteps, and we both stood out of respect as Killian's three older brothers entered the room, trailed by at least a dozen attendants. I didn't think there was a complete outfit between them all.

"Brigance. Ronan. Kier." Killian nodded his head at each of them, greeting them out loud for my sake as well. I'd only met the trio once - Ignea had tended to keep all her children behind the scenes in subservient roles most of the time I'd known Killian.

None of these males had been through the sort of ruinous treatment as him, though. I'd often wondered what strength they must possess if Kills had been rejected as the runt of the family.

"Brother," Kier said, his face breaking into a grin

as he reached to shake Killian's hand. They shared a certain similarity in looks, though Killian had told me before that none of them had the same father. Ignea had ruled Aralia solo, preferring a string of lovers instead of giving any measure of power to a king.

"What brings you here?" Brigance asked, his tone flat and polite. As the oldest, he probably would have replaced Ignea and become Aralia's sole king if the deal of shared power hadn't been bartered with the Council, in exchange for increased Aralian representation in Patriam.

On the surface at least, Brigance didn't seem to resent his reduced position.

"Our Queen of Haret wishes to visit Aralia," Killian announced, jumping right to the point. I saw his shoulders tense in anticipation of protest. Indeed, I was surprised when none of his brothers corrected him regarding Carlyle's status.

The three fae before us simply nodded and murmured their assent - even Ronan, the second-born brother who I knew as the most dangerous. Prickles of intuitive warning danced along my spine - although none of these fae had ever been as cruel as Ignea, this sort of mute acquiescence was very, very unlike them.

Killian glanced back at me, and I caught the same glint of mistrust in his golden eyes.

"She would also like an audience with Marcel while she is here," I added, and three pairs of eyes shifted to me. Again, all the brothers nodded without even questioning why Carlyle might be in need of a fae doctor.

"We are in Queen Carlyle's debt," Kier said, and the other two nodded again. I frowned, suddenly pinpointing the reason their behavior bothered me: it was as though they were puppets, heads bobbing on a string. But who could possibly be the puppet-master to three such strong fae?

Something was certainly up.

"Aralia is open for our Queen at any time. We will prepare the rooms at once," Brigance added, and the three of them gave brief bows and stepped back, vanishing behind the gauzy curtains with their half-naked cotillion. Killian and I were left blinking at each other.

"That was fuckin' weird," Killian growled. "But I'd rather question Marcel than any o' them."

"Perhaps the good doctor has medicated them," I said, chuckling. The doctor hadn't even made it to our meeting, brief as it had been. Killian snorted and held out his elbow.

"That would be fuckin' genius. Take us home, mage. We're gonna need the vampire's skills for this one."

CHAPTER THREE

SOL

Damn me to the darkness if I wasn't secretly glad Tilda had shown up and stirred Carlyle up. The minute Jack and I had exited the library behind her, she'd yanked the two of us into her bedroom.

"Goddamn, baby," Jack murmured, his voice slightly slurred. She'd taken us both immediately, Jack in front and me behind. Her movements were fierce and claiming, like she was making a point to someone. We'd rested, tangled in a lazy mess in the sheets for a few hours.

Now she was at it again.

"Greedy Qilin," I teased her, tucking a lock of hair

behind her ear as she finished licking Jack's cock clean. We'd all gotten more used to sharing the bed with each other, but I got a special sort of satisfaction from watching her with another man.

"You have no idea, lion," she shot back, climbing over Jack and reaching for me again. "I feel so hungry," she added in a whisper.

"Want me to send for some food?" Jack asked, not moving a muscle or even opening his eyes.

"Maybe later," she said, laughing at his limpness. "I mean hungry for my mates. It's like my body is afraid…" She trailed away, frowning. "No, afraid isn't the right word." She shrugged, sliding her hips across mine and stroking my cock back to full attention.

"I'm not complaining," Jack said, a lazy smirk on his face as he watched her move across my body, his eyes heavy-lidded.

Unlike Killian and me, Jack preferred to keep his eyes on our pale goddess, though. I wondered idly if Jai would consider another round of what he'd done with Killian and Carlyle not long ago.

Then she sank her tight pussy onto my cock, and I stopped thinking about what wasn't in the room. Carlyle leaned forward and braced her palms on my chest, kneading at my muscles.

"Mine," she growled, her voice stealing a bit of my roar. Her hips rolled over mine like a tidal wave, and I groaned as I took her passion. It was all I could do to hold her down as she bucked and swiveled, grinding herself harder and harder on me.

"Fuck," I panted, barely able to draw breath as she bore down on me with all my own lion's strength. All too quickly, I felt the dizzying pressure build at the base of my spine, and I was helpless beneath her. I came with a hoarse shout, and her body gripped me like a fist, claiming every drop for its own.

Her eyes churned a deep purple in the darkness of the room, glinting as she gazed down at my panting chest with a look I could only describe as gloating pride.

I grinned up at her, and one corner of her mouth hooked up in a smirk as she swiveled her hips one last time, wrenching another groan from me.

"I've worn you two out," she murmured, glancing over to where Jack had passed out, his breathing soft and deep. She brushed her fingertips across my eyes, urging me to do the same.

My lids were heavy enough, and I was losing my last hold on consciousness. Sleep had nearly claimed me when I felt her slide off my body.

I tried to lift up to follow her, but damn it if she wasn't right. As she slipped into the hallway and disappeared, I sank back into the pillows, telling myself I'd talk with her a little more tomorrow.

None of us were exactly complaining about this new level of insatiability, but I had to admit our Qilin goddess had changed recently.

KILLIAN

I'd been sleeping like a baby - a restless, whiny baby who has no idea what it really wants. So, of course I heard Carlyle's soft steps padding down the stone hall toward my room.

And just like that, I knew exactly what I wanted. I'd pretend to be surprised when she shimmied into bed with me with those cold-ass toes of hers.

Calming my muscles into stillness, I feigned sleep as she slipped inside.

My air magic had its own ideas, though. She smelled like sex and Sol, and before I knew it, I was caressing her beautiful curves and the heat between her legs with the tiniest bit of breeze. I felt the vibrations in the air when she shivered, but she didn't move to close the open window.

Instead, she gripped the edge of my light blanket and ripped it off me in one smooth movement.

"Fuck," I cried, no longer pretending to be surprised.

"Your Queen is in need of your service." She smirked as she swirled the blanket around her bare shoulders and stared down at me regally. Her hair glowed nearly silver in the moonlight.

"Oh, I'll service ya," I growled, glancing down at my hardening cock. Naturally, I was already naked and more than ready for my girl. The muscles in my chest and abs were clenched against the sudden cold, and she surveyed my body with a slow, satisfied grin that made me proud as hell. "Come here, Qilin."

I reached to haul her on top of me, but she darted away from my fingers, instead climbing nimbly up the other side of the high bed. She knelt over my hips, shifting her weight to one knee while the other propped up to open herself to me.

Naturally, she was already naked too.

Now, I could tell she smelled of the lion *and* the dragon, but that only perked me up a little farther. So, two men and she hadn't been satisfied yet? Looked like I had some blessed work to do.

The blanket draped open around her curves, and as the moonlight spread its pale magic across her skin, she looked every bit the magical Queen and Goddess she was to all of us.

Until she grinned. Her lips curled up in a wicked invitation, and my cock jerked against my stomach, aching for her warmth. My girl wasn't about to stop leading the show, though.

She stroked her palm along her inner thigh, keeping her eyes fixed on mine the whole torturous time. Her goddamn challenge stare wouldn't even let me back down and watch as she dipped two fingers inside her wetness.

Knowing she'd already been filled by Jack and Sol and still needed me…that was a pure shot of lust.

The tip of her pink tongue peeked out to run over her lips.

My tongue mimicked the movement, and I would

have toppled her and delved deep inside her mouth if she hadn't reached for my swollen cock just then. She spread her silky moisture across my tip, toying with my piercing as she went.

"Canna believe I have ya all to myself," I whispered, grasping her ankle and stroking up the back of her calf.

A slight shadow passed across her face, and I immediately regretted my words. I knew it must be hard balancing the six of us, and if it weren't for her demanding, ravenous nature, I would be getting a lot less of my incredible mate.

But my savage Qilin shoved her dark thoughts away in an instant, returning back to that mischievous smirk.

Without warning, she sank her body straight down on my shaft, and light burst behind my eyes. I groaned, and I heard her giggle as my hands locked around her thighs, pinning her. Of course, it didn't make a bit of difference - she was still very much in charge.

Her hips ground down on me, pressing my cock impossibly deep. She swiveled and undulated, pushing her palms so hard into my chest that the air escaped my lungs in tiny puffs.

Carlyle let go of the blanket as our bodies heated, and it slid down her shoulders to pool around our legs. Her skin was like liquid lightning against the shadows of my room.

Her fingers slid between mine on her thighs, then

she suddenly flattened her chest to mine. Her teeth snapped at my neck, which was as far as she could reach in her bound position.

"You little beastie," I teased, as she pried my fingers away from her legs and yanked my hands up past my ears.

Her grin was barely more than a slice of warning before she began to really move above me. My Qilin set a galloping rhythm, and within moments, both of us were panting and close. She freed me, and my hands barely knew what to do, running in wild lines up and down her soft body as she rode me toward oblivion.

Just as the pressure began to build unbearably along my spine, and my legs tightened in anticipation, my girl's pale form flashed dark above me. My eyes bugged wide as her silvery blond hair went black as night, and her skin became a shadowy contrast.

"The fuck?" I grunted out, blinking as the effect disappeared. She murmured something, but then her eyes slid up and her lids closed in bliss as orgasm shuddered through her.

Her body sucked at mine, tipping me over the edge, but I strained to keep my eyes open. And there it was again. Like seeing the negative of a printed photograph, her human glamor slipped away for a split second.

Except it wasn't her Qilin above me, horn flashing. I'd seen that a time or two, and it was always a mix of awe and terror.

But this. This was new.

She was a dark goddess above me, eyes glowing solid white in black skin, ebony hair flowing like electricity around her as she grinned wickedly, pointed teeth snapping. She was a mix of vampire, dark fae, and something else my mind feared to name.

"Fae?" Carlyle whispered, tucking herself against my chest and wrapping her arms under my shoulders. "What's wrong? You're shaking."

Raising my head, I blinked down at her, my heart beating even harder than our activity warranted. Curled into the curve of my shoulders, she looked small and soft and normal again. What the fuck sort of mind tricks was my brain pulling? Maybe I just needed some damn sleep.

"Ah, ya got me good, Savage," I managed to confess, the breath still shuddering through my lungs. She grinned and nuzzled into my neck, and with her warm touch, the fear began to fade.

The problem was, I wasn't even certain *why* I'd been afraid. It seemed more like the edge of a nightmare now, fading into the forgetful darkness of sleep.

"Your Queen is satisfied with your service," she murmured, her body sliding off mine so she could curl deeper into the crook of my arm.

I tightened my arm around her waist in response, tugging the blanket back up and over both of us. Her breathing evened out within moments, and though mine did eventually, sleep never came for me like I'd expected.

Instead, my mind turned that dark image over and over all night, wondering why it felt so alien yet so familiar all at once.

CHAPTER FOUR

CARLYLE

Despite the urge to yank one of my guys into the shower with me, I locked the door and tried to steam away my nerves in silence.

I wasn't about to admit to any of them how much I needed to hear Dr. F's answers or theories about me having babies. Ah, a baby. *One*. Not plural.

Damn it. I hadn't been able to think of much else. Even my body had taken over the fucking refrain - literally. It was like a little voice in my head begging to mate my mates every four-point-three seconds.

A couple of months ago, when we were cooped up on the beach with the Underbelly kids, I hadn't even wanted kids. Hell, I was still terrified of the idea.

But even if that leprechaun hadn't actually cursed me, he'd gotten me good by planting a seed about that first-born crap. The mind was a powerful thing, and mine was currently obsessed.

I should have been way more worried about the darkbloods and Tilda's reports of rebellion.

But fuck it all, as though there was a rip tide in the ocean of my mind, I was forever being sucked under imagining what it would be like to have a baby with one of my mates.

Fighting free of those thoughts yet again, I quickly dressed. Instead of fancy dresses, ball gowns, robes, and crowns, I'd designed my queenly attire mostly around the idea of an assassin queen. If it was tight, black, and made of leather, I was into it. Around the castle, I preferred leggings, or, ah, nothing. But when I was dressed to impress?

Yeah. Ass-kicking attire it was.

Dair had even ordered a gorgeous pair of thigh-high boots from a mage armory shop in Patriam, and I grinned as I smoothed the buttery-soft leather up my legs. The low heel hid a compartment where mages often stored a token of their elemental magic to give themselves a quick boost.

I just enjoyed the sharp click of the boots on the stone floor.

I strutted into the massive kitchen where I knew my guys would be gathered for breakfast. We loved eating family-style with all the shifter staff and whoever else was around.

Tilda was still there, and she looked less than impressed with the whole homey atmosphere. "Perhaps that's where the eradication rumors started," she muttered, surveying my outfit.

I narrowed my eyes at her, but I kept my lips sealed. Since when had I ever cared what a mother-in-law of mine thought? Wasn't about to start today.

I grabbed a piece of toast and spread sweet jam across it, accepting a steaming mug of coffee from Toro. He leaned in for a kiss, snagging a bite of my toast after he finished.

I set the toast on his plate and drained the coffee. I wasn't really hungry, anyway.

"So, Aralia? Let's make this quick, yeah?" I said lightly, glancing at each of them.

Jai nodded. "Toro and Sol will stay here to monitor the castle."

I knew Toro was also being tasked with keeping an eye on his water beneath the water, or whatever the hell he was calling that discovery. It sounded cool on the surface, to be connected to some kind of underground river. But no matter what fun it might bring, it was still a weak spot in our fortress.

Of course, Dair and I had spelled the crap out of it.

But it didn't take motherly instincts to be hyper-protective about my guys, not to mention all the Haretians living in the castle with us. The world of Haret was newly mine to protect, but my citizens never let me forget for long that not all of them wanted my protection.

"I'll be heading back to Patriam presently to calm the masses," Tilda added, but nobody even acknowledged her except Dair.

After kissing his mother politely on the cheek, my mage held out his elbows to Jai and Killian, and I grabbed hold of Jack.

Locking eyes with Killian, I visualized the great hollow-tree hall of Aralia in all its fae glory, trying to keep the distaste and distrust out of my mind while we traveled through the cosmos.

"We'll stay in Aralia as long as you need." Jai assured me as we all popped into the main reception room of Aralia's carved palace.

I scanned the space nervously. The last time I'd been here, Killian and I had ah, *performed* for a huge crowd of fae to make a point to his mother.

I felt my lip curl at the memory, but Killian pressed close behind me. His strong hands gripped my hips and pulled me close.

"Everything is different, Savage. You'll see," he whispered. "My brothers aren't like her."

On cue, three male fae as large as Killian strode into the room, their shirtless bodies boasting a gorgeous mix of pale blue skin and black tattoos outlining a king's ransom of muscles.

I blinked, reeling my thoughts back. What the fuck, Qilin? Checking my body, I found that it hadn't actually responded to them at all. That was damn good because I had absolutely no plans for more mates. My stomach actually sickened a little as I repeated that to myself.

Nope - it was my guys and me forever after - nobody else.

But my brain was still on its tangent that it didn't hurt to appreciate the scenery, right? Whoever snagged these newly minted kings would have some fun.

I heard Jai snort next to me, and his hand slipped around my waist, weaving past Killian's arms and gripping my hip along with the fae. Jack tugged one of my hands between his, twining our fingers together. The three of them touching me and each other gave me more than enough distraction to forget about the other fae.

Jai gave me a knowing sideways grin. *Look at anything you want, Qilin. We know you're only hungry for us,* he whispered in my mind. My skin flushed as I realized I'd been caught ogling the Aralian kings.

But for once, Jai didn't seem jealous. Instead, he twined a contrasting tendril of his icy power down my spine. I heard Killian's breath stutter too, and I knew he was feeling the cold against his lower belly.

Dair gave me a sideways smirk, as if he were thoroughly enjoying my tight spot.

I know you're mine where it counts, my vampire hissed in my mind, and I had to bite back a moan as his magic spread across my hips, prickling even lower. Killian was growing hard behind me, and for a split second I was ready to forget about Dr. F and siphon us all straight the hell back to my royal bedroom.

"So this is the Queen of Haret?" one of the fae said, interrupting Jai's wandering hands and my dirty thoughts. I flushed even harder. He'd been studying me as well, though he looked more amused than anything.

"Carlyle, this is Brigance," Killian said, stepping slightly away from me and gesturing to the fae. "My oldest brother. That one's Keir, and that's Ronan."

I tried to remember if I'd seen any of them before, but that whole night had been an absolute blur of fear and power plays. I didn't even know what sort of fae magic Killian's brothers might have.

Keir smiled nicely enough at me, but Ronan remained blank-faced. It wasn't exactly a rude look, but I didn't feel welcomed by him, either.

But I needed to focus - get my baby-making answers and get home so we could figure out how to deal with the rebellions.

I nodded to each of them, starting to feel awkward for a whole other reason now. I mean, I'd *murdered* their mother.

I opened my mouth, trying to think of something queenly to say, but words were scarce. The awkward silence grew to epic proportions.

"Carlyle!" a voice rang out from the side of the room. Breathing an overly obvious sigh of relief, I turned to see Dr. F striding toward us, a real smile on his craggy face.

"When we first met, I never thought I'd be glad to see you," I joked, remembering the trials he'd put me through in the Council's lab on Earth. Not to mention the ugly things he'd reportedly done to the other Qilin.

But we all had regrets, right?

Marcel smirked and nodded to me, holding himself in his black lab coat as regally as any king might. He paid no attention to my four guys, and I noticed that he was also basically ignoring his three kings. That small fact made me giggle, and I bit my tongue to stop it.

Focus, damn it, I reminded myself again. What was *with* my brain these days?

Killian cleared his throat, saving me from yet another awkward pause. "Brothers, if you'll excuse us, our Queen has lots of questions for Marcel. We'll join you for dinner if you'd like." He offered his arm to me, and I took it, noting the slight increase in his formality.

My fae was as uncomfortable as I was, which was ironically comforting.

"Of course," Brigance replied. "We will command preparations." With that, the three kings turned almost in unison.

"Follow me," Marcel called, already halfway across the room, heading back in the direction he'd come from.

As we hurried to catch up, I caught a glance between Jai and Killian, but their thoughts were blank to me. I could tell something was weird in Aralia, and I wondered if Jai had taken the liberty of skimming thoughts from its new kings. Regardless, I knew he would prioritize our issues with the darkbloods.

We really didn't have time to take on any more mysteries, even if it was Killian's family.

Dr. F led us briskly through several winding halls, all carved from the interior of the massive tree that housed Aralia's royal family. Finally, we reached a more clinical office space, with freshly painted cream walls and soft chairs.

"I wasn't exactly given much information on why you're here. Is this a private consultation?" he asked, eying the four guys who had taken up most of the space.

"Ah, maybe?" I replied, realizing I hadn't thought that far ahead. "Yes," I amended, straightening my shoulders. "Sorry, boys, but I don't want to be distracted. I'll tell you everything when we're done."

"No tricks," Jack growled at the fae doctor, who only sniffed as if such a suggestion were ridiculous. And it was, really.

"This Qilin needs no threats to protect her, nor does she need any of you," Marcel drawled, swiveling on the ball of one foot and opening a nearby door for me. I nodded to my four mates, noticing Dair was especially steely-eyed.

"It's fine," I hissed again, glaring at them and turning back to Marcel. When we were in the next room with the door closed behind us, he raised his eyebrows at me.

"Still being coddled, are you?"

I shrugged, leaning against a counter. Now that I was here, I wasn't exactly eager to jump up on the exam table.

"Things are a little, ah, strained," I admitted, wandering the small room. I wondered what exactly Marcel used for his practice here. There was no visible equipment, and I knew Earth tech disintegrated quickly in Haret.

He studied me intently until I settled into the wheeled chair that was probably meant for him.

Crossing my arms over my chest, I sighed and looked up at the good doctor. "That fucking leprechaun gave me a few things to think about." I told the whole story again, catching him up on the basics and ending with the stupid riddle. "He said: *When darkblood runs, all shall mourn. All hail the Queen, and her first-born. But rue the night, and rue the day, When the balance tilts, the secret's sworn.*" I hung my head back and rubbed my temples. "So now, I'm wondering *how* I can have a first-born."

"Do you *want* a first-born? Or are you trying to prevent one?"

Goddamn it - he'd cut right to the chase. I felt my skin heat, and Marcel chuckled.

"There's no shame in either one, my Queen. But I admit, I have no ideas on how a Qilin could conceive without a Qilin mate. Granted, I'm not an expert in treating your species, but I've studied all the medical books in Haret. There are no documented cases of that happening."

"Well, I'm not taking another mate," I said, the words coming out a little fiercer than I'd intended. Marcel's lips hooked up in another amused smirk.

"I'd say you have your hands full," he agreed, and I didn't need my filthy, busy mind to fill in the rest of the places I was keeping full.

"Can you at least tell me about, ah, Qilin pregnancy?" I bit my lip, feeling shy as hell and hating it. I wasn't thirteen in sex-ed class, for fuck's sake.

"Well, Qilin typically have one foal at a time, though it's not unheard of for twins or multiple births. Anecdotally, I've heard that Qilin spend much of the brief pregnancy and birth process in their true form." He shrugged and spread his hands. "Don't you have a mother you can ask?"

I glared at the floor. I certainly did, and I certainly wasn't ready to go there with Neva. Really, I was afraid I'd take whatever she said too personally. I didn't exactly blame my mother for all that had happened, and she'd had a damn good reason for the things she'd done. But still.

"If you really don't know anything, I'll try her next," I conceded, sighing through the words. Even I was getting tired of my sighing, but I couldn't seem to stop doing it.

"I'm happy to examine you," Marcel said, gesturing to the table that I was still pretending didn't exist. "In Aralia, we use our elemental magic to test fae for illness. My fire magic is more useful in surgery, unfortunately, but I could call a water fae and an air fae if you like. Together, they work a bit like Earth's medical scans. Or, you could siphon me back to the Path, and we could commandeer an exam room on Earth."

His eyes sparked at that idea, and I sensed a bit of the bloodlust it seemed all fae possessed.

"Ah, let me think on it. After dinner, maybe," I answered, realizing I needed to check with Killian about inviting any other fae. Not for permission exactly, but to see if he trusted his people enough with whatever intel they might learn from a scan of my body.

I trusted Marcel, but he was the extent of it.

Marcel nodded. "In the meantime, I may have an anatomy book," he offered.

"Yeah, sure," I agreed. It couldn't hurt, right?

There was a knock on the door then, and Marcel moved to open it. Killian filled the doorway, and I could glimpse the rest of my guys crowded in the room beyond.

Seriously. It had been like, fourteen minutes.

"Our rooms are ready. An' they're providin' the goddamn clothes again. My brothers have a show to put on for their subjects," he added, rolling his eyes.

"I figured as much. It's kinda like my payment for coming here," I said, shrugging. We'd been through that plenty of times in Patriam. It was a Queen thing, evidently.

I gave Marcel a little finger wave and followed my guys down the hall.

"Anything?" Killian asked, giving voice to what all of them wanted to know.

I shook my head. "Not really. He told me to ask my mother - which is a hell no for now, so don't even bother asking. And he offered to have a couple of fae scan me for illness."

I sensed Jai's spike of icy power at that suggestion, and I hadn't even gotten to the idea of going back to Earth. I smirked at my vampire. He was such a possessive thing. I also heard the whisper of the question I'd told him not to ask, but I ignored it. He wasn't the only one with mommy issues.

As soon as we were locked up safely in the suite, I turned on my guys.

"Now look, I know you're all worried. I'm okay, I promise. And I need to know what my body can do - that's always been the goal. Right, Jai?" I asked him pointedly, since I could feel his protective doubt searing me even without dipping into his thoughts.

I flashed him an old memory - something he'd known had happened but hadn't been there for. The very first time Sol and I had fucked, my lion pinning against the cement wall in the training room. Sol had been insistent in promising me I couldn't get pregnant by him or any of the team, and I'd believed him.

Jai growled deep in his throat, but he didn't contradict the intel, either. As far as anyone knew, I really couldn't have a first-born with any of them.

And to be perfectly honest, I would have definitely shown up preggers by now if it weren't true.

"Cariño," Dair said, sighing. "We're as confused as you are. None of us know anything more about this than you do."

I nodded. "But Marcel might be able to figure something out if you guys can stop the whole overprotective bullshit act. I want those fae to scan me," I said, fixing each of them in my stare and ending with Jai for good measure. "Do your icy worst after they're done if you feel the need to seal their minds. But I need to have someone help me figure this out."

Dair stepped toward me, gathering me in his arms, and I felt Jack's hand slide across my shoulder to cup the back of my head. Dair said, "We'll figure it out. Don't worry about the fae."

"Or your mother," Jack added, kissing my temple. "We can even make a visit to Earth. There are still plenty of Haretians in the medical field there who we could utilize."

"Boss, I want ya to ice those fae," Killian said, leaning heavily against the door and crossing his arms over his broad chest. His face was hard. "My brothers were never the problem - only my fuckin' mother. But somethin's wrong here, and I donna trust anyone in Aralia right now."

Jai nodded. "I feel it, too. Your brothers are not themselves."

"Wonderful," I said, plastering on a beauty-pageant smile. "So, let's use our time before dinner. Kills, go tell Marcel to round up the two fae he mentioned. You and Jai can talk to them and come get me when you're satisfied."

For a second, it looked like Jai wasn't going to agree, but then he nodded. Without a word, he strode out of the suite, Killian hurrying to follow.

CHAPTER FIVE

CARLYLE

Some part of me hadn't expected Jai to actually approve the scan, and I was nervous as crap to finally be in the narrow exam room again. It was hella crowded, too.

Marcel was sort of standing guard near my head, with a water fae and an air fae at my left and right. Jai was hovering near my feet, and even Dair had been brought in.

I glared at Jai, letting him know silently that I fucking knew his game and I could damn well siphon myself out if things got weird. The vampire only stared blankly back, and I huffed.

For that matter, I shot at him in my mind, *I have enough magic to torch the entire room. And Dr. F knows it.*

But he didn't budge. Instead of fighting, I rested my head back on the crinkly exam room paper and forced myself to relax. "Do it," I said, rolling my eyes at how much drama we were all creating around this stupid riddle.

The air fae was a tall, slim male who proved that not all fae were insanely attractive. He hovered his hands a few inches above my head, then slowly moved them down my body without touching.

The only thing I felt was the sort of prickle you get when you sense someone behind you and the hairs on your neck stand up. It was so light I wondered if it was in my imagination.

Reaching my toes, he glanced at Dr. F and sort of shrugged.

"N-nothing, sir," he stammered, and I cracked a smile. The fae was terrified of Marcel. Of course, I could reason out why.

"Nothing what? Nothing wrong? Or…" I trailed away.

"Nothing out of the ordinary," Marcel answered, waving the fae away with impatience and pointing to the other one. "You. Begin."

The water fae nodded. She was even more timid than the male, and I had to wonder if Marcel had picked them this way. Either that, or his reputation was just as bad with his own people.

As the rose-skinned female moved her hands in a

similar way, I actually noticed a fluttering beneath the surface of my skin. It reminded me a little of Toro's water magic, and I wondered if maybe Killian and Toro could be taught how to look for whatever these fae were searching for.

That would be handy. Of course, if the training took years like Earth's medical schools, it wouldn't be very practical.

I caught the fae's eyes widen as she passed over my chest and stomach, but she controlled any other reaction until she was done.

"What?" I snapped, beating Marcel to the question. He narrowed his eyes at me, then the fae.

"It is her *sruth*, sir," the water fae said, her voice nearly too quiet to hear.

"My *what?*" I demanded. The small fae startled and shrunk away from me, though, and I could tell by her lowered eyes that she wasn't about to answer.

"*Sruth*," Marcel repeated. "It's the energy in your body. The flow of magic through your cells. Human medicine where you're from does not widely acknowledge it, but it's perhaps the most important piece in the puzzle of any creature's health."

"And what's wrong with mine?" I continued. I'd had my fair share of trouble accessing my magic in the past, but nothing recently.

"It's…muddled," the fae said, sounding confused.

"*Sruth* gathers in key places in the body, and each place has a certain significance. They are found above the heart, between the ribs, and near the lower belly, for example," Marcel continued, gesturing toward the areas the fae had seemed to notice.

Something about this was sounding familiar, but I couldn't quite place the intel in context. "I'm still stuck on this idea of it being muddled. Like when I mix things up?" I was trying to be vague, because I didn't want to subject these poor fae to any more of Jai's mind-eraser magic than necessary.

Marcel seemed to catch on, and he ordered them both away. Jai trailed behind them like a predator.

As soon as the door was closed, Dair stepped between us protectively. "Marcel, I have something more," he said. I sensed him speaking with Jai, though he kept his thoughts locked up tight. When I caught his navy eyes, I saw an apology already forming.

"Cariño…there is something Jairo and I thought would complicate things."

I took a deep breath, not wanting to fight with my mate in front of Marcel. But really. "Seriously, Dair?" I muttered. We'd been over this secret-keeping thing a time or two.

"I'm sorry. We were both in agreement that it would make things harder for you until we knew the significance. But the clues may be coming together. We found a heartstone," Dair said, looking at Dr. F.

The fae doctor's eyes lit with fire. "Where?" he hissed.

Dair slid his fingers through mine. As I sat up, he wrapped an arm around my shoulders. "Cariño, I found it after the leprechaun died. It was in the same vault where I'd stashed the gold coin. *Instead* of the coin," he added, and I frowned.

"Who would have replaced it?" I asked, feeling like I was missing something.

"I believe the coin was a heartstone all along, simply under glamor so we wouldn't recognize it."

Marcel growled low in his throat and stalked to the other side of the room, as though he would prefer to be out of the cramped space.

Whirling on me and answering the questions already on my lips, he said, "Heartstones are used to open your heart *sruth*. To cleanse it of this…muddled quality. Which I do suspect is the result of you mixing magic to create new skills," he added.

"Is the *sruth* like *kardia*?" I asked, uncertain how this all fit together.

Dair shook his head. "As you've seen, a *kardia* is a physical container for your magic. *Sruth* is concentrated energy."

"Isn't all physical matter made of energy?" I was in over my head with my unfinished high school education, but I'd read that in one of LuAnn's stolen library books on new-age topics. Suddenly, my brain fetched the context it had been searching for, and things clicked. "*Sruth* are like chakra, aren't they?"

Both men looked at me, uncertain.

"Chakra are studied on Earth, but not that much where I was from. They're energy centers. In places like the crown of the head, the forehead, the throat, right?"

Marcel nodded, a smile growing on his face. "So you do know."

I grinned, nodding. It was a relief to have my context. "But why are you so worried about a heartstone? Cleansing is good, right?"

"If it was indeed disguised as the coin the leprechaun gave you, then it was quite a message. It would mean your heart *sruth* is blocked or damaged. And, more significantly, that someone knows about it," Dair explained.

I frowned, still not on board with his concerns. The riddles pointed to a huge secret - some blocked chakras didn't exactly seem like an issue of national security.

"Could anyone scan me without me knowing it?" I wondered. Maybe we needed to focus on that part.

Marcel tilted his head. "Doubtful. It's rare for a fae to be able to scan your air or water without being within a few inches of you."

I sighed. Yeah, I would have noticed that.

"And leprechauns do not have the magic necessary to do the scan, correct?" Dair asked. Marcel affirmed it with a nod, staring into the distance.

"There is another possible test," the doctor suggested, his words slow and contemplative. "We could summon an energy fae."

Dair sucked in a breath, his eyebrows raising. The door opened just then, and Jai came slinking back in. His expression was blank, but the mated part of me sensed the remnants of his ice magic. He'd sealed the memories of both fae.

"I thought energy fae were a legend," Jai said, settling at my other side. I sank into my mates' shoulders, relieved by their constant support. If I had to figure out all this shit by myself, I'd be so lost.

"They are a carefully-guarded secret," Marcel corrected. "And they are incredibly rare. I know of only one living near enough to be of use. I could summon her, and you could possibly see her in the morning."

I looked up between Jai and Dair. They both nodded, and I shrugged. "I came here for answers. Might as well try another route." Especially since I didn't feel like I'd actually gotten much yet. Sure, it was weird that me mixing my magic had blocked my chakras. And it was creepy to think that someone knew what was inside my body even better than I did.

But I still felt like we were missing some pretty vital pieces to the puzzle.

"In the meantime, eat well and enjoy whatever show the Three Kings have prepared for you," Marcel suggested, a small smirk on his face. The thought that he could be the one acting as puppeteer in Aralia crossed my mind once again, but Jai pulled me down from the table and out of the exam room before I could even respond.

"Damn, I hate doctors," he growled as we made our way back to the suite.

"Well, I know you're practically immortal, but the

rest of us occasionally need a tune-up," I teased him.

"No, Carlyle. You're perfection. There is *nothing* wrong with your body," he purred, pressing me tight against the door to the suite.

I rolled myself into him and arched my neck, offering my lips up for a kiss. Just as he began to taste my tongue, the door opened behind me, and I sort of fell backward onto a hot mess of fae muscle.

Killian's arms closed around my middle, and Jai's hands cupped under my thighs, pulling my legs securely around his waist. Killian slid his grip to my ass, and I relaxed into the embrace as they walked me inside the suite. The door clicked shut behind us, but I barely noticed.

"This is better than a lollipop," I murmured, finding myself reclining onto Killian's chest on the bed while Jai worked his way from my mouth to my neck. Kills didn't seem to mind being my chair, and I found it to be an advantage when his fingers gathered my shirt up around my collarbone. Jai's fangs traced the line of my neck, and I moaned softly, craving the thrill of having him bite and suck at my fluttering veins.

He didn't though - Jai preferred to keep that sort of *aima* pleasure just between the two of us.

Instead, he inched his way down until his mouth was pressed over the place where I guessed my *sruth* was in trouble. He kissed it tenderly, and I felt the barest prick before his tongue gathered whatever tiny droplet of blood he might manage.

"It's her *sruth*," he whispered, and I felt Killian tense beneath me.

"Marcel is calling an energy fae," I added, arching into Jai's lips. I didn't want to talk. But my words only made Killian more fidgety, and Jai evidently sensed it, too. He raised his head and looked at my fae, and I felt like a child trying to catch their silent conversation.

"I need to speak with him, then," Killian said, lifting me out of his lap and settling me on the pillows. I started to pout, but Jai pinned me with a scorching look.

"Don't worry. I'm not leaving," he whispered. With a movement so fast I barely saw it, he yanked down my leather pants. I gasped at the lingering pinch on my skin, but the noise turned into more of a hum as he settled between my thighs. Jai was masterful in that position, and as a bonus, I got to muss his long, silky hair while he worked.

His tongue and fingers brought me to a moan of release way too soon. He sat back on his heels, grinning like a fiend who'd just convinced a mortal to sell her soul. His hair hung like a black curtain of silk over one shoulder, and I rolled my eyes at how quickly it had fallen back in place. Mine would have been a nest of tangles after that.

"What about you?" I asked, reaching for him.

He only smirked and slid off the bed. "I know humans get suckers at the doctor. Marcel was fresh out, so I had to improvise."

"Damn, I love it when you joke." I grinned, even forgiving him when he stepped farther out of reach.

"I need to check on Killian. Perhaps after dinner we can finish what I started." His eyes raked over my half-undressed body still splayed where he'd left me.

"You got it, boss," I replied, giving him a saucy salute as he sauntered out the door. He looked pretty pleased with himself, and I kinda loved it.

I peeled down my boots and shimmied the rest of the way out of my pants, then went to the bathroom to freshen up. When I came back wrapped in a soft robe, Dair was sitting in a chair, one ankle propped up on his knee.

"I doubt it's much help, but Marcel did give me this," Dair said, offering me an anatomy book.

I flipped through it, rolling my eyes at what were essentially someone's notes and hand-drawn illustrations of Qilin bodies.

"Tibor had more knowledge than this," I complained. Of course, since the Enforcer had ripped apart the KeepSafe pod holding the Qilin captive, there was likely nothing left to learn in the underwater kingdom.

I was getting a sinking suspicion that I was going to have to find my mother.

Feeling discouraged as shit, I handed the book straight back to Dair. I knew he would scour it without needing any help from me.

"Let's just get dressed for dinner. Eat some good food, have some sleep, and hopefully that energy fae will be here in time for me to get checked out in the morning," I said.

"We'll figure this out, Cariño," Dair whispered, standing and folding me into his arms. I leaned into him, breathing deeply of his silky, sharp scent of champagne and tobacco. He didn't stay, though, and soon I'd been left alone to dress. I spent way too long struggling with the filmy material and spiderweb straps of the complicated dress the fae servants had left for me to wear.

Finally, I surveyed myself in the mirror, pulling a few curls off my face and adding some deep red lip stain from the gift basket on the counter. There was a circlet of delicate white flowers, too, and I twined it around my official crown. The crystals gleamed in the softly lit room as I surveyed myself and smiled.

I liked being barefoot, too. Some of the fae wore outrageous heels, but many of them loved the feel of their soles on the forest floor.

Aralian fashion was so different from anything I'd normally wear, but I always enjoyed the dramatic, sexy flair of it.

"Damn, I'd almost forgotten about those pants," I murmured as I strode into the main room. My guys had finished dressing, and I was ready to appreciate the hell out of my shirtless men in their Aralian leather pants. "Those laces, tying your cocks in all tight and shit." I reached over and tugged at Jack's laces, and he hummed, his eyes going molten.

"Your dress isn't half bad, either," Dair said,

turning heavy-lidded navy eyes on me. He looked the most startling in the getup, and something in his gaze told me he wouldn't mind a bit of costume play one of these days.

"Yeah, I like ya in half a dress," Killian agreed, giving me an appreciative nod. I grinned and linked my arm through his.

The dress whispered around my legs as we moved down the hall toward the great room. It was moss-colored and clung to my curves like smoke, dipping low between my breasts and barely crossing my shoulders. My back was bare, and more than one of my guys gave into the temptation to run his fingers up my spine, tracing my moon and stars tattoo.

KILLIAN

I could tell Carlyle had zoned out during the meal, and I was relieved. I didn't want her focusing on whatever fuckery my brothers were up to. The show being put on for us was some sort of history play, but even I couldn't make sense of the goddamn thing.

I found myself studying my brothers instead, cataloging the many ways they seemed odd or different.

I hadn't spent real time with them since before my mission to Earth, though, so I could just be reading the whole thing wrong. It was possible they were just pissed at me for any number of reasons.

Keir was being nice enough, though it sounded hollow. Brigance kept starting to say things then snapping his mouth shut, like someone was pinching him under the table. Ronan was less of an ass than I remembered, which was plenty weird in itself, since he rather prided himself on that shit.

Studying Brig while he gave instructions to a servant fae, I hit on it. It was their eyes. It didn't really make sense, but they were just too damn bright, like they'd been drinking more than the light dewberry wine that had been served all night.

Like they'd been drinking something more ancient and more magical, like whatever my mother used to serve when she was doing business with a particularly difficult adversary who she couldn't afford to simply kill.

"I need another fucking drink," Jack said, leaning toward my ear. I snorted and snagged him one. "This is bullshit, you know," the dragon continued, watching as Carlyle was guided toward shaking hands with yet another high-ranking fae. "Why does she always have to parade around like a goddamn prize pony?"

"She's a Queen now," I muttered, knowing it was a bogus excuse. Everyone in Haret wanted a piece of our girl now, and we all fucking hated it, especially her. They either wanted to gawk at her - the Qilin who had restored the Path and turned into a Goddess - or they wanted some shit favor from her.

She had more power than any creature in our history, and every one of us would rather hide her away than let anyone get their fucking claws in her.

Still, Aralia was going to be a problem again, one of these days. The knowing sat in the back of my mind like a snake coiled in a basket.

Jai looked over at me, and I felt his ice creep into my brain. *Forget about your family, fae. We do nothing for the vampires, the fae, or any other fucked-up kingdom in Haret until Carlyle is safe from this darkblood trouble.*

Not a problem, boss, I answered in my mind, knowing how much it cost him to add his own kingdom to that list. Sure, I was curious and dreading the fallout from whatever was happening here, but in reality, I could walk away from this place forever and not look back.

My girl would hate that, though.

As much as she avoided her own mother, Carlyle valued family, and she desperately wanted us all to keep our ties to our families and kingdoms.

CHAPTER SIX

CARLYLE

Something in the drinks the fae kings had given us had made me too sleepy to enjoy my men, and I woke up damn grumpy because of it. What a waste of lace-up pants.

The others were still sleeping soundly, so I stomped into the bathroom, cursing whatever tricks the fae might be up to.

As the hot water and flowery soaps soothed me, though, I realized we'd probably just overindulged. I didn't need to have them *every* night, after all. My silly body didn't have to mate at every turn.

Feeling much calmer after that mental massage, I

stepped out of the shower, wrapping my long hair in a towel. I hummed to myself, enjoying the yummy lasting scent of the fae beauty products. I'd definitely have to grab a few bottles of whatever this was.

Turning toward the mirror, I raised my hand to wipe away the steam and froze.

What the absolute *fuck*?

Words were scrawling themselves on the mirror like in a cheap horror movie, appearing letter by letter in the thick steam. I stumbled backward into the wall, clutching another towel to my bare chest like it could protect me.

A panicked glamor scan of the open room showed I was completely alone with these magical words. Well, alone except for four highly sensitive and severely overprotective men who *should* be waiting just on the other side of the bathroom door.

Men who, except for their sound sleep, should be finely attuned to the fear blossoming in my chest right now…

The door burst open, and a tiny scream escaped my open mouth.

Jai lunged for me, checking me over frantically. "I felt…I heard…" His thoughts were as disjointed as his words as the rest of them crowded into the space. I huddled against Jack and pointed silently at the mirror, watching the steam drip and distort the letters.

As the line faded, the steam sort of regenerated, and more words appeared. It looked for all the world like someone was drawing them right before us. The air popped with magic as Killian and Dair scanned and found nothing.

Silently - well, actually, with a lot of muttered cursing - we all watched until the rhyme was complete. I saw Dair had procured a notepad and was copying down the lines, but I knew I'd remember the words forever.

One Queen and her six Kings
Dragon's fangs and Vampire's wings
Oracle's sweetness speaks too loose
A Prince or Princess rules all the things

"What does it all fucking mean?" I groaned as the last line faded. I was feeling the binding sense of frustration creep in. I loved a good bit of wordplay, sure. But these stupid riddles had too many loose ends - too many infuriating interpretations.

"Dragon's fangs and Vampire's wings?" Dair repeated, frowning down at his paper. "That should be the other way around."

"I doubt it was an error," Jai hissed, but Dair only raised an eyebrow at the vampire's rage.

"Is the Prince and Princess bit still about your first-born?" Jack asked, scratching his chin.

I resisted the urge to snap back that I had no fucking clue. He was probably right.

"Why would they rule instead of you?" he muttered.

"Anyone know an Oracle?" I asked, ignoring that

and pushing through my men and heading to the bedroom. I dropped the towels and yanked on my black leather - no more filmy dresses for this girl today. I had shit to kick.

I sensed Jai's answer before he pushed it into my mind. *I know of several oracles. But one is of particular interest to me, after yesterday's session with Marcel. She's rumored to be an energy fae as well.*

"Well, let's go then," I said, turning to him and offering the nicest smile I could manage through my annoyance.

"She's in Paris," he added aloud, glancing back at Dair, who had both eyebrows up now.

"Okay, damn. I'm definitely in now," I replied, feeling a little better. "I've always wanted to go to Paris. They have chocolate croissants there. And café au lait."

"I know, *aima*. I know," Jai whispered, crushing me in his arms and holding me tightly enough that I knew he was very, very worried.

I probably was, too, underneath all this vibrating rage.

But for now, I was just a girl-shaped pile of molten lava seeking something to fucking burn.

My guys were in action mode, too.

Killian was already roaring down the hallway, and I could hear him shouting for his brothers to begin an investigation immediately. That was a good point - how had that magic made its way into our suite? Jai's ice magic crackled through the air, and Dair nodded, siphoning away instantly.

I rubbed my temples, lacking the motivation to even ask Jai where he'd sent my mage.

Jack was systematically tearing the suite apart, searching for any signs of an intruder or magical residue.

And Jai…Jai was staring at me with an intensity I should have been uncomfortable with.

Instead, I was just numb.

"It's always something," I muttered, finger-combing my hair into a messy, wet braid.

"Carlyle," Jai said, then stopped, as if he wasn't sure what to say either.

I just shrugged. It wasn't anything new. Not really. There would always be threats against a Queen, especially a Queen like me, whose very existence threatened so many people's ideas of their own rights to rule themselves.

This time, it was just extra-complicated because of the whole weird pregnancy thing.

"So, are we going to wait for Dr. F's fae? Or split?" I asked, my hands propping on my hips.

"Dair has gone to Marcel's quarters to inquire. Unless she arrived in the night, I don't think we should wait."

I eyed the vampire. "Actually, I don't think we should wait at all. Let's take care of this ourselves. Maybe I was wrong to bring us here. Call Dair and Kills back."

To my surprise, he nodded. Within seconds, Dair

popped back into the suite, looking mildly annoyed.

"The fae hasn't arrived yet, anyway," he told me, shrugging.

Jai huffed, as though he'd expected as much. Really, I had, too. Even a royal summons didn't usually have instant results. He told Dair, "You wait here for Killian. Carlyle will take Jack and me back to the castle."

Jack was by my side in a second, and I trusted the boss's orders. I didn't want to spend a second more in Aralia than necessary.

Of course, when I popped us back into the throne room and realized Tilda was still hanging out, I couldn't help but sigh.

"Have you left Alisdair in Aralia?" she asked, her eyes narrowed.

"He's a big boy. He can siphon himself," I snapped, wondering why she'd stayed.

"No news, then?" It wasn't really a question, and I ignored her sourpuss expression, looking around for Sol and Toro instead. My lion had been lounging on a couch beneath a sunny window, but as soon as our eyes met, he rose and prowled toward me.

"Missed you, shortcake." His arms wrapped around me, and I breathed in his calming, summery scent.

"It's only been a night," I murmured into his chest. Still, I could feel the stress of the visit shaking through me as he held me close.

"Let's have a powwow over breakfast, yeah?" Jack

called, his light steps already heading in the direction of the castle's massive kitchen. I grinned against Sol's shirt, thankful that no matter what was going on around us, I could count on Sol to be sweet and Jack to be hungry.

And Jai to be surly, I added, as he stomped after Jack.

We were nearly out of the throne room when Dair and Killian siphoned in, and they fell into step with us. Soon enough, we were all seated at a rough-hewn wooden table spread with the best shifter pastries and jams, fried meats, wedges of homemade cheese, and platters of exotic sliced fruits found only in Haret.

I hummed in satisfaction, digging in. Sure, my life was constantly being pitch-forked by the outside world, but when we were just home with each other, everything was pretty amazing.

Dair murmured a containment spell around the table just as Toro slid onto the bench across from me. This ensured our conversation would be blocked from any of the shifters working in the kitchen around us. It was a protection for them as well as for us - if threatened, they'd have no information worth spilling.

"Handy," I said, grinning at Dair over a huge bite.

"You have no idea," he answered, his dark blue eyes heating with a promise I hoped we'd have time to fulfill soon.

"Tilda, this intel stays here," Jai warned her, bringing me back to the intensity of what we were facing.

She nodded. "Of course. Thank you for including me. Patriam's resources are at your disposal, should you need them."

I smiled. She was a prickly thing, but of all my in-laws, she was the main one we could count on to help us at least as much as she protected her own country. That was worth a lot.

"So, we have three riddles now," I began, feeling like I needed one of those huge whiteboards they always had in police dramas. "One dead leprechaun. A bunch of pissed off darkbloods who think I'm going to commit genocide. Blocked chakras - ah, I mean *sruth*. Some kind of heartstone that could heal that. An Oracle to find and question. And no proof, but just an odd feeling in my belly that I really could have children, if we decide that's what we want."

The last bit was practically whispered. I'd barely admitted as much to myself, much less my mates.

I heard Tilda suck in a breath and hold it. My mates were silent for once, and I felt their nerves strumming the air around me, almost like the buzzing of insects on a summer night in the south.

"One more thing," Jai said, and I thought I saw a hint of flush across his cheeks. Dair tensed beside him, and I groaned.

"Secrets? Fucking really?" I shoved half a pastry in my mouth to force myself to stop griping.

Jai continued, his eyes fixed on the table before him. I felt a little better realizing how bad he felt.

"You mentioned the leprechaun told you he was called Harold. But I don't believe that's a name."

He looked at Dair, and my mage nodded, taking over. "Harold is not a Haretian name. But with the inclusion of an Oracle in this latest riddle, we are certain this leprechaun was actually a *herald*. The sort of messenger that Iaga and her magic would task with receiving a prophecy, delivering it, and seeing it through to its conclusion."

My mouth was slack as I took in this turn of words that should have been obvious to me. I mean, master of puns over here.

But then the end of his explanation smacked me in the face. I slumped down, my forehead narrowly missing my plate.

"Goddamn it," I muttered. "He can't see it through because I fucking shanked him."

Again, the silence was telling. I'd screwed up.

"But why would Iaga go to all this trouble with a prophecy and a bunch of riddles? Why wouldn't she just come tell me whatever she needs?" I asked. Sure, the goddess had sort of gone radio silent once I'd taken the crown and the castle. But I knew she was still around.

"Maybe a darkblood group stole the prophecy and is using it to force your hand," Tilda suggested. I frowned. It was possible, but there were a lot of holes in that explanation. Like, how did you steal a prophecy? And why go to so much trouble?

"Perhaps Iaga's magic isn't strong enough to take

her full form now," Toro suggested.

Nobody else offered a suggestion. Toro's didn't feel right to me, either. Iaga had assured me that she would never completely leave, just that she was fading as I was rising. Like how the moon waxes and wanes, or the stars fade out when the sun is shining. A transfer of power.

That last bit stuck in my mind.

She'd transferred lots of power to me, for sure. But what if there was more? I'd been so concerned with avoiding the darkness before. Maybe I'd sucked too much light from her.

"Maybe I need more balance," I murmured, pushing away from the table and pacing. I ignored the questions my guys began throwing at me, blocking them all out with the mental equivalent of hands over my ears. I might have even been singing, "La, la, la."

The darkbloods were worried that I was coming for them. To eradicate them.

I wasn't, but I knew I'd been terrified of darkness before, thinking it would make me like Aleron or the Ringmaster. If others had picked up on that fear, it didn't take much of an historian to connect those dots.

They were likely terrified of the lightbloods and their obvious political advantage.

I had the rainbow, but black was a color, too, right? If I was going to rule both light and dark, maybe I needed to get more in touch with my own darkness. Understand it. Integrate it, even.

I slid my eyes to Jai. Who better to explore this idea with than my sexy, dark-minded vampire?

"Take me to Paris, boss," I whispered beneath the louder conversations around me. His eyes widened, the black beginning to bleed into the white in the most delicious way.

CHAPTER SEVEN

JAI

Of course, I wanted to take my sweet Qilin to Paris. But the danger…

Her voice slid into my mind. *Take me, boss. This is the next step. I feel it. You know I can't hide out here forever - what kind of Queen would I be if I ignored whatever this is?*

I sighed, knowing in my heart that she was right. She angled her body to face mine and began to stare me down. I felt the others in the room grow quiet, watching our silent battle.

Her mind circled mine, inserting more thoughts meant to soothe. The sly thing was learning to beat me at my own game. *Jai. Come on. You and I are two of the most powerful beings in Haret - or Earth for that matter.*

A faint smile tugged at my lips. She was goddamn right. I knew I coddled her unnecessarily - I needed to protect her more than she needed to be protected.

But in certain moments, I could admit that I loved her most when she was by my side, fierce and fearless.

Silently, I gave in and answered her. *I'm just deciding whether to bring the team or keep that sweet Qilin body all to myself in the city of love.*

Obviously, we were heading to Earth for a recon mission and not the pleasure trip I would have much preferred. But the look in her wide lavender eyes told me she had all sorts of extra activities in mind.

Fuck me, I was in trouble.

Her lips quivered as she tried to suppress a grin. She knew she'd won. In my head, she offered, *Take Dair if you think we need backup. He can siphon anywhere on Earth to get help if we need it.*

Fine. But only him. I don't want to keep track of anyone else, and that Oracle is skittish, I answered her, molding my face into a scowl I didn't really feel. I flung a thought to Dair to get our things ready, and he siphoned away. Fastidious fucker would need a moment to pack.

Staring the rest of them down, I sent the plan into each of their minds. I knew they'd hate the arrangement, but I didn't particularly care. I'd skimmed Carlyle's thoughts a bit, and although I suspected she'd allowed me to do it, I didn't like her idea of opening herself to the darkness.

It would be a delicate thing to balance, for sure. The fewer of the men who were around to influence her, the better.

I turned to Tilda. "Expect a report back in two or three days, max. Do your politician thing and keep the darkbloods quiet. Our Queen harbors no ill will toward them unless they seek to harm innocents."

She nodded, her eyes flicking to Carlyle.

"I know words are cheap," Carlyle said, sighing and tilting her head back to stare at the ceiling. "But please give them my word and reassurance. I have to earn their trust, I know. I'm just not sure how to do that yet."

"It just takes time," Toro said. "Everything moved so fast once we opened the path."

"Yeah, baby," Jack added, drawing her close to him. "Give things a chance to settle. You'll bring everyone together, just the way you did with all of us."

Sol reached for her fingers across the table and squeezed, smiling at her. They were good men, and I knew I was as lucky as Carlyle to still have them around.

Dair strode back into the room in time to catch the end of the reassurance. He nodded. "Yes, Cariño. Haretians will easier trust a constant supply of small deeds and gestures, rather than a single grandiose one or promise."

Carlyle smiled, though it looked a little weak to me. "Thanks, guys. I appreciate the support, and I know it takes time. But it would help a lot more if I could just keep my fucking horn out of any more of them," she added with a scowl, crossing her arms over her chest.

"I took the liberty of packing for you as well," Dair murmured in her ear, redirecting her attention with ease as he held up a light brown leather satchel. I didn't miss the arch of her eyebrow, and I hoped the mage had remembered to pack something appropriate to visit the Oracle, and not just a stash of his favorite lacy underthings.

Tilda nodded to us and siphoned away as the rest of the team crowded around Carlyle to say their goodbyes again.

Each of them gave me a warning glare too, but I took it in stride. I would keep her safe. Whatever it took.

CARLYLE

"Welcome to Paris, Cariño," Dair murmured as the three of us siphoned into an alley just off a crowded street. I'd already half forgotten our serious business in my eagerness to explore.

"I promise we'll take time to visit the city, *aima*," Jai said, taking my elbow and leading me smoothly into the crowds. "But first, we need lodging."

"Is this the Champs-Élysées?" I asked, my jaw

dropping as we merged into the throngs of people. At the far end of the wide street, the Arc de Triumph loomed, looking even more massive than I'd imagined from pictures. Shop windows lined both sides of the street, promising purses and shoes as expensive as some cars. The cars themselves were a mass of heated traffic, with tinny horns blasting as they crept along in snaky lines, refusing to obey traffic laws.

"It is," Jai affirmed. I strained against his grip, my nose twitching at the scent of coffee and croissants and gorgeous perfume, and so, so many humans.

"Damn, there are so many emotions here," I said. It had been a while since I'd been around so many people, and suddenly, I felt more than a little overwhelmed. I sagged back into Jai's arms and let him guide me as my senses adjusted back to the odd sensation of smelling hundreds of emotions along with everything else.

"Lodging first," Jai repeated, nodding at a balcony ahead. We ducked into a building, and my heart skipped a beat as my vampire launched into a fluid stream of French.

Dair chuckled as he glanced down at me. "Didn't expect that, did you, Cariño?"

"Fucking hot," I whispered, mesmerized by Jai ordering up a room for us on the Champs-Élysées - in fluent French.

Damn vampire had too many secrets. As I followed him up the stairs and into a narrow hallway, I reflected on how much I had to learn about all my men.

I knew the important things, of course. But I was so glad I had a lifetime of little surprises like this ahead of me.

The room was absolute perfection. All gilded and fancy and so Parisian. There were a pair of high, carved beds - tall enough that I might need a boost. An ornate dresser with a large mirror lined one wall, and I could see the edge of a claw-footed tub through a half-open door.

The balcony, though.

Jai pulled the heavy drapes aside and gave me a gentle push toward the glass-paned double doors. They opened wide, without any screen to block the breeze. The bustle of the crowds below drifted gently up to me, and I leaned far over the railing, drinking it all in.

"I love it," I whispered, knowing Jai would hear me.

And I love you, Jai answered in my mind. He joined me on the balcony and hugged me from behind, his mouth nuzzling the base of my neck. *I want this to be perfect, but I know we have work to do. Forgive me?*

I twisted my face down and met his lips, answering him with a leisurely kiss. Slipping him a promise of my own, I assured him we'd make the most of every second…just as soon as he returned.

Jai sighed as he ended the kiss and stepped back from me.

"Mage, stay here while I visit the Oracle. She

doesn't take well to new faces, and she's just as likely to turn us away as see us." Jai's face was a mess of scowls again, and I frowned.

"Are you sure I shouldn't just come with you now?" I asked. I was impatient to see her, and I had sort of a gut feeling Jai was worried about nothing. Intuition was telling me we were in the right place, and that we'd get some answers this time.

"No. Stay with Dair. I'll bring home dinner," Jai added, a sly smile on his face.

"As long as you bring dessert, too," I agreed, raking my gaze up and down his finely-muscled form. I winked, resting my eyes at his waistline.

"Take care of her, mage. After all, Paris is a bucket-list for her," Jai growled, flashing me a hint of fang that thrilled me all the way up and down my spine. And then he was gone in a blur of vampire speed - I barely even heard the door open and close again.

"So, how are you going to take care of me, mage? After all, this is Paris." I repeated, swiveling to Dair, who was locking the door again behind Jai. We were in the most romantic city on Earth, alone for a few hours. Surely, the mage had a plan.

Dair stared down at me, one side of his slow smile hooking higher than the other, giving him the most delicious, roguish smirk. "I plan to fuck you senseless, of course."

My body jerked like he'd run an electric shock through me, and I sort of tripped forward into his arms.

"That'll do, I guess," I mumbled as he bent his neck and pressed his lips to mine.

Dair's kiss was so encompassing that I hardly noticed him slipping the clothing from my body as he walked me toward the bed.

"You taste so good," he whispered, as we bumped into the high mattress. He lifted me under the arms and set me gently on the bed, placing my face level with his. His fingers tangled in my hair, keeping me close as we breathed the same air and our tongues tangled in a pace that was both slow and greedy.

I opened my thighs and wrapped my legs around his, urging him closer, but of course, he had other plans.

Letting go of me and stepping back, he reached into his jacket pocket and withdrew a handful of dark fabric. Holding it high, he allowed the fabric to slide between his fingers and tumble into my lap.

I bit my lip as I realized it was a length of raw silk, unfurling all the way to the floor. "The better to tie me up with," I murmured, and the man in front of me grinned like the big bad wolf.

"On your knees, love," Dair said, his voice as soft as the silk he was now trailing across my shoulders. I obeyed without question - this was my mage, and I was about to be a very good girl.

He turned me away from him and pulled my arms slowly behind my back, sliding the silk beneath them. "Tell me if it hurts, or if you wish me to stop, and I always will."

Knowing he would, but that I wouldn't, I slid my eyes closed and tried to picture what he was doing. The silk pulled my arms closer across my back, and I felt him loop it over again and again, then the jerk of a knot being tied. I flexed my muscles and found I couldn't move much with only my normal strength.

Dair looped the silk again, this time crossing it over my stomach and back again a few times, then around my wrists, binding my arms to my body as well. I bit down on a giggle as I realized I would totally faceplant if I lost my balance now.

"Beautiful," Dair murmured, his fingers strumming the bonds. "Search my mind for the image," he suggested, and I did.

"Wow," I whispered, admiring the black silk tied tight across my pale skin. "That's crazy sexy, mage."

"You have no idea," he said, his voice more of a growl than usual. "Turn your head, and I'll lay you down."

He slipped an arm around my shoulders and lowered my body gently to the bed. Resting on my stomach, I could just barely glimpse him over my shoulder as he stripped out of his button-down and slacks. His weight dipped the bed behind me, and he pulled my hips up just enough to slip a pillow beneath my stomach.

"Looking for that good angle?" I teased. He chuckled, and his fingers slid between the pillow and my core. I hummed a little as he stroked my folds, circling my clit with a gentle fingertip and spreading my wetness. Then something hard and cool pressed against my skin, and as his fingers withdrew, I heard a click.

"Oh, fuck," I moaned, as a mild vibration began on my clit, pressed tight between my body and the pillow.

"Absolutely senseless," Dair repeated, clicking the vibrator off again. Then he grasped the silk that linked my wrists and my waist, pulling my hips up a few more inches so he could add a second pillow. To my surprise, the vibrator moved with me, like it was stuck to my skin.

This was some next-level mage shit, evidently.

But then his cock was nudging against my entrance, and I moaned as he pushed inside me so fucking slowly. I tried to push back on him, but his hold on the silk kept me fairly still. Even when my knees slid a little on the duvet, he just braced his knees behind my thighs and torqued my hips up with the silk.

I was at his mercy, and I knew I was going to love every fucking second.

He was barely all the way in when he started a slow withdrawal, and I was nearly whimpering like a drug addict. I clenched my jaw to keep the noise inside, though. I'd be a good girl if it killed me.

The next thrust was every bit as slow, and I was cursing him inside by the third time. My arms ached a tiny bit, but I was not quitter.

Dair switched to rapid, shallow thrusts that left me panting against the duvet, and then I heard the click a split second before he pinned me to the bed, going so deep in my core that I lost what little breath I had left. The vibration on my clit was relentless as he held my bindings tight, fucking me with his special brand of dark mercy.

Maybe I'd been right to bring Dair along on this quest, too.

Then he was backing away, clicking off the vibrator and teasing me with his tip again.

Goddamn it. So this was the game.

I gave in to the rolling sensations, holding my shaking body together as best I could and letting the silk do the rest of the work. At some point I finally lost grip on my focus and orgasmed so hard I felt like I was levitating in Dair's grasp. The vibrator mercifully stopped, and I was completely boneless.

Dair let go of my arms and grasped my hips, grinding into me, his thighs slapping the back of mine. We were both slick with sweat, and I was trembling with the aftershocks when he finally shouted his release. He slumped over me, kissing my mouth sloppily from the backward angle.

"Senseless," I whispered, and he chuckled, out of breath. He rolled to the side, staring into my eyes.

"You were quite the good girl," he purred, his fingers tugging on the knots of silk. He procured a warm cloth and a small vial of rose-scented oil, and he worked to clean me, then soothe any place the silk had rubbed at my skin. I sighed into the massage as he started to rub the oil into every bit of my body.

The afternoon sun had begun to slant into shadows before I thought to ask about Jai, but Dair only shushed me, his hands kneading the oil deep into my muscles until my eyes drooped closed in a light, blissful late-afternoon catnap.

CHAPTER EIGHT

DAIR

Carlyle was still napping lightly when Jai finally slipped into the room through the balcony. From the angle, I guessed he'd come from the rooftops, like a proper parkour vampire.

He set a bakery box and a few white paper sacks on the little breakfast table and beckoned me onto the balcony with him. I left the French doors open, but I pulled the heavy drapes closed to keep the room dark for her.

"The Oracle's missing," Jai said, not mincing

words.

"Fuck," I breathed, leaning over the railing. "Why am I not even surprised? Any ideas?"

Jai shook his head. "I checked all the places I've found her before. Nobody's talking." He crossed his arms and gazed down at the throngs of people. There were still just as many humans streaming in and out of the shops, crowding around the Arc de Triomphe, and packing the streets with their tiny, idiotic cars.

"Let me try," I offered. "I still have contacts here. Diplomats. Perhaps I can get farther." I didn't say what I was thinking, but we both knew it - Jai was intimidating, and unless he flexed his power, it was more likely for someone to clam up than offer intel. "Enjoy this time, boss," I said, quieter this time. I certainly had taken advantage of the few hours alone.

He cracked the edge of a smile. "Twenty-four hours max," he agreed. "If you haven't found anything by then, we'll go home and look for another lead from there. It makes me nervous being away from Haret. I don't want this to be a goose-chase while something happens behind our backs."

I nodded grimly and slipped back into the room. Pulling my jacket from the chair where I'd discarded it earlier, I pocketed the length of silk. Not that I needed it - but I felt the desire to keep my Queen's sweet scent with me as long as possible. I slid the bolt from the door and stepped into the hall, taking the stairs like a normal human might.

Pressing my way into the throng, I contemplated

where to go first. Haret had consulates in major cities, just like the humans. Sometimes they were even housed in the same building. But not in Paris.

I made my way down a side street, taking the turns from memory until I came upon an ancient church. This was no tourist attraction, though it predated many of the city's more famous attractions. In fact, it was glamored to appear under construction to keep away the uninformed.

Knocking on the wood sparked a shower of magic that I knew would only be visible to a Haretian. The shields were up, and the security was actually a relief. As the door dissolved enough for someone to see me, I felt the subtle tingle of my body being scanned by a spell.

Anticipating the coming question, I spoke up readily. "Alisdair Baxtrom. I hail from Patriam, in Haret. I served as a junior Council member until accepting and completing a mission to find the last Qilin. She is now Queen of all Haret, and I come on her behalf. We are looking for someone in Paris," I added, hoping this branch of the Council had been kept up-to-date and wasn't one of the outliers who still thought the Path was closed.

Or worse, one of the holdouts for the darkblood rebellion.

CARLYLE

The room was warm and dusky when I finally blinked open my eyes. Someone was on the bed with me, but the scent was all vampire. I didn't sense Dair anywhere in the room.

Stretching, I rolled over and saw Jai reclining against the velvet headboard, his shirt unbuttoned and his dark, silky hair loose around his shoulders. He lowered the book he'd been reading to smile at me, and my whole body sighed with the picture he made.

I didn't care why we were really in Paris - I was the luckiest Qilin in the damn world.

"Hey, you," I murmured, sitting up and leaning into his shoulder. I tried to smooth my hair back and rub the sleep from my eyes. I probably looked a mess, but the look Jai gave me was so soft. His full lips hooked up higher on one side in a sweet smirk, and his fingers tangled with mine as he pushed my curls away from my neck.

"Did you nap well? Are you hungry?" he asked, leaning down to kiss me gently.

I sort of murmured an answer, but I was more concerned with my vampire than with food for the moment.

He broke away and grinned, brushing his thumb over my cheek. "I brought pastries from my favorite Parisian bakery - I've shopped from three generations of them now."

Okay, maybe I was a little concerned with food. If Jai had been visiting the same bakery for that many years, it must be impressive. And weird, but I was slowly getting used to the idea of us being basically immortal compared to humans.

Jai slipped out from under me, propping me in the bed with the extra pillows, and darted to the little café table in the room. He flicked the heavy drapes open a few inches, and I saw that while it wasn't night yet, the sun was definitely on its way down.

"I slept too long," I said, frowning. I didn't want to miss any more time in Paris. But then a box of fresh French pastries made its way into my lap, and all disappointment was forgotten.

Jai chuckled, pointing and naming them for me. "Raspberry mille-feuille. It has vanilla custard. These are madeleines. Tarte au citron - the best lemon flavor I've ever had."

There were so many, and while I recognized some of the words, I was pretty much content to listen to his voice and that sexy as sin accent he'd revealed.

"What's this one? It's gorgeous," I murmured, picking up a small, round cookie-type pastry that was a delicate lavender color. There was a tray of six, all in beautiful violet shades. A tiny purple and white violet was molded on the top of each one.

Jai grinned, and I could tell I'd picked his favorite. "A violet macaron. Of course, I also have pain au chocolat - your chocolate croissants. But when I saw these macarons, I thought of your violet magic. And it's honey-flavored, so that reminded me of you, too," Jai added, smirking.

I snorted, but after one bite of that crunchy, velvety macaron, I was a convert.

"These are real violets!" I pulled the flower carefully off the pastry, tasting it. It had been flattened and sugared, so really it was just like candy, but there was something so fresh and spring-like about it. And mixed with the sweet honey flavor?

"Fucking heaven," I moaned, my eyes rolling back as the cookie dissolved on my tongue.

"I'm glad you like them. I managed to skim the recipe from the old woman's mind, so we can make them at home," Jai boasted, and I swear, I wasn't even mad that he'd taken advantage of someone's sweet Parisian grandma.

He opened a paper sack and pulled out a jar crammed full of what looked like honeycomb. He held it up in the slanting rays of sun, and I saw violets preserved in the jar, too. "I couldn't resist this, either. I wanted so much to cook for you in Paris, my *aima*. But time is short, so again, all I have are promises."

I caught his jaw between my palms and kissed away the frown that was beginning. "All I need is you - I don't need cooking or even promises of cooking. Besides, we're practically immortal. We can come to Paris every fucking year if we want to."

"And so we will." Jai gathered me close and took over my kiss, stealing any further words from my lips with his heady taste and the delicate scrape of fang along my bottom lip.

"So where have you sent Dair?" I asked after a few lazy minutes. I sank back into the pillow and accepted a bite of the lemon tart. As much as I wanted to see Paris, I couldn't deny the appeals of this hotel room.

Jai's hesitance made me twist up on one elbow and stare him down, though. His lips turned down in what I would have called a pout on a lesser man. On my vampire, it was straight broody sexiness.

"I am sorry, *aima*. The Oracle is missing."

I sucked in a breath. Goddamn it. "And Dair is looking for her," I finished.

Jai nodded. "He has Council contacts here who are more likely to speak to him than to me."

I smiled despite my worry. Yes, Dair did have a way of smoothing things over that Jai certainly lacked. "So, missing like she went on vacation and didn't tell anyone? Or missing, like foul play?"

Jai's face darkened. "Her home had been broken into. The scent of blood was there, though I didn't see any spilled."

"This can't be coincidence," I said, and Jai shook his head in agreement. "I wonder if this is part of the riddle, or if there's another group working against the first group like Tilda said, trying to keep me from figuring things out. It all makes my head hurt," I said with a sigh. We were having enough trouble with the riddles and the darkblood implications. Thinking there was a second group out there we were racing against made me grouchy as fuck.

"Dair will handle it. For now, shall we see Paris?" Jai asked, picking up on my mood instantly.

"Is that really the best idea?" I asked, wanting so much to say yes, but curious as to why Jai would be the one advising a distraction. He was usually so cautious and work oriented.

"I do work too much. Yes, I heard that thought, *aima*. I told Dair to take twenty-four hours. I'm planning to do the same. Besides, we both know we could handle a bit of danger," he added, a light growl to his words. I eyed him for a moment, then grinned, liking his new attitude.

"What the hell. Show me Paris, boss."

For once, we spent the late afternoon and early evening like pure mortals. We took the stairs and the sidewalk and the metro, and we paid for coffee with euros. We sat in sun-dappled gardens, fed pigeons, and petted the dogs being walked before dinner. We smelled the flowers and tossed our remaining coins in the Seine.

And finally, we made our way across the bridge to the Eiffel Tower I'd been eying all day.

Standing in the courtyard, I craned my neck like all the other tourists. "I suppose you've been here more than once," I said, staring up at the massive metal structure above us as Jai pressed behind me and circled my shoulders with his arms.

"I was here when that glass elevator was a spiral staircase," Jai whispered against my neck, pointing at the elevator taking people up to the various levels.

"It's over a thousand feet tall, though some of that is the antennae. We'll go all the way to the top level, unless you're frightened."

I felt his smile against my skin, and I turned my head to meet his lips. "I'm in, but I have a special request. I may not be a member of the mile-high club, but my bucket list includes me staring down on the lights of Paris with you deep inside me."

I received a little nip on my bottom lip for that one, and I sucked it inside my mouth, lifting my eyes. Oh yeah. His eyes were starting to bleed black.

"We'll need to come back after closing for that, *aima*. In the meantime, what else would you like to see?"

"Show me your favorites," I suggested. We wandered away from the massive tower, and I expected to be taken to the Louvre, or one of the famous churches.

Instead, Jai ducked into a narrow alley between buildings and led me a few blocks from the hubbub.

"Old Paris," he murmured, spreading his arms wide before wrapping one arm around my shoulders and hugging me close to his trim body. Even though the day had been sunny, the night was turning cool as I snuggled into his embrace.

We walked slowly through the narrow back streets, while Jai murmured stories in my ear.

"We spent so many years split apart on different missions. Each of us began to gravitate toward certain areas that reminded us of home in some way. Paris was mine."

I frowned to myself. What I'd seen of Saori Sang - from a massive distance, of course - didn't strike me as very similar to the cobblestones and balconies around me.

"There are dozens of places that look more like Saori Sang, or smell like it, of course. But the soul of Paris - beauty, love. The lights. The *food*. That's why this city reminds me of the best parts of home. That's what it was like when my mother was alive, and when Grand-Mère ruled. It wasn't cold and dark and cruel like Merden has made it."

His words ended on a growl at his aunt's name, and I wrapped my arm around his waist.

"We'll handle that, Jai. I promise."

He hummed in agreement, but I could tell he was done talking about it. Instead, he led me through an artists' district, where the street vendors were packing their paintings away. We window-shopped the glass-fronted boutiques and ducked into a bakery just before closing, buying their last brioche stuffed with ham and gruyere, and paper cups of rich dark coffee.

There were still cafés and bars open, of course, but we chose the Seine instead, strolling along the dark water as we ate. If I'd still thought I was human, it might have seemed a foolish thing to do.

Even the latest danger hinted at by our riddled chase might have made us hesitant and cowering.

But as I gazed up at the lights of the city melting into the stars farther above, I sensed nothing could touch us, not really.

It was a heady feeling, when there was normally so much danger. Knowing what I was, and walking hand in hand with a vampire who remembered nearly a hundred years' worth of this city, I suddenly felt truly immortal.

Whatever this new quest threw at us, we would manage, my men and I.

Long past the cathedrals had struck midnight with their booming chimes, we made our way back to the base of the Eiffel Tower.

"Think it's abandoned now?" I asked, excited but thinking how awkward it would be to run into a security guard.

Jai dropped a kiss on the top of my head. "I recommend some glamor - I'm sure there are cameras. But I'm sure you can siphon us away in the blink of an eye," Jai suggested. I grinned. Yeah - Dair had taught me that much.

"Hold on, vampire," I murmured, staring intently at the top level and its enclosed viewing area. I took a long moment to visualize our landing, then pulled us into a siphon.

The top of the Eiffel Tower was fucking breezy, but damn, was it exhilarating.

I pressed my face to the metal enclosure, peering down the dizzying height to the city spread before us. Jai crowded behind me, his hands running up and down my sides to warm me against the wind. I spread a glamor of invisibility over us, adding a layer of sound-blocking magic just in case.

Jai leaned in next to my ear and pointed ahead. "Back that direction is our hotel - you can see the Arc de Triomphe. Across the river there are the Trocadéro Gardens we walked in. Down the river that direction is the Louvre. Can you see the glass pyramid?"

I nodded, though now that we were finally up here, I much was less interested in the sparkling lights below us than in the vampire pressed against me.

"Has it always been this beautiful?" I whispered, arching my neck to the side as he trailed his lips along my skin.

"Always. Though I've never been here like this - with my beautiful, powerful mate. My *aima*."

His hands slid softly down my sides before he grasped my hips and wrenched them back into his. His cock was like steel against my ass, and there wasn't much in the way of fabric between us.

Soon there was nothing, as Jai pushed my dress up and my lacy panties down. I widened my legs and leaned into the railing as he caressed my bare hips with touches that alternated between light as air and possessive massage. His knuckles grazed along my ass and between my thighs, maddeningly close to my most sensitive areas.

I pushed my hips back a little farther, sucking in a breath as he slid his fingers along my slit, spreading my wetness.

Jai's hands circled my waist and pushed my dress

higher, bumping up my ribs. He tugged the cups of my lace bra down and teased my nipples, which were already hard in the cool air.

His hips pressed tight against my bare ass, and I cursed his fully clothed state, but I kept still and allowed my vampire to seduce me exactly the way he wanted.

Jai's fingers pinched my nipples as he leaned over and kissed down my spine until he reached the moon and stars tattoo. His tongue swirled over the magical ink, and I moaned as lust twisted deep within me.

His lips slid farther down, until I felt the scrape of fang follow the curve of my ass. And then Jai was kneeling between my legs, his face tilted up to my pussy.

"Oh, fuck," I breathed as his tongue teased my clit. My thighs trembled as I tried not to squeeze them together over his face, and I heard him chuckle. Then his lips closed around my clit, and stars burst behind my closed eyelids. I'd barely caught my breath before he was standing again, unbuckling his belt.

His thick cock pressed between my thighs and entered me from behind, and I sighed in satisfaction as he stretched me to my limits. My body was still pulsing gently around him, and he whispered my name as he began slow, shallow thrusts.

Leaning over my back in an embrace, Jai continued to kiss and nip along my shoulders, neck, and jaw. His hands fisted my breasts, rolling my nipples between his fingertips.

There was absolutely no rush to his movements, only a steady, assured rhythm that built and deepened until the end was as inevitable as the moon in the sky above us.

"Jai," I whispered as I came again, my body trembling against his.

"I love you, my *aima*," he answered, pressing himself as close and deep as our bodies would allow as he came with a growl that vibrated all along my spine.

I didn't know how many minutes I stared down at the city, basking in the yummy afterglow.

But eventually, the chilly air began to wind its way into awareness. Jai slid my dress back down, and I tugged my panties back into place, giving him a satisfied grin and another kiss.

Jai just hugged me close and whispered, "Siphon us back to the ground. I want to show you something."

I didn't hesitate, but I was surprised to find us siphoning straight into a gathering crowd.

I'd barely opened my mouth to ask about it when light exploded above us. The whole tower was instantly lit from top to bottom with glittering golden lights, its massive shape cutting through the dark clouds.

"Wow," I said, laughing and grinning up at the shining landmark. "Glad we weren't up there when that started. It's beautiful," I added, snuggling into Jai's chest as he locked his arms over my shoulders.

"You'll have this beauty again and again, I promise," he whispered, and I sank into him, happier than I'd ever been.

CHAPTER NINE

CARLYLE

"I was hoping to find you alone." Jai's deep, growly voice slid across my shoulders. I just grinned and set down my coffee.

He knew damn well I'd be alone up here. He'd planned it that way, leaving that note tucked into a fluffy white robe, pointing me to the rooftop garden after a luxurious rose-petal soak in that gorgeous claw-footed tub.

We were the only ones up here watching the sunrise, which I was certain was also by design, but no complaints from me.

I selected a raspberry from the tray of fruit he'd

just deposited on the round café table. Using my tongue to burst the berry in my mouth, I sank into its bright, fresh flavor. And then Jai's lips were on mine as he stepped across my lap and leaned over me. My hands trailed up his thighs, feeling the tight muscle beneath his dark jeans.

My fingers hooked into his waistband, but his kissing grew fiercer, distracting me from playing any games. His hands tunneled into my damp hair, caressing my neck and tugging at my curls. His mouth consumed me, kissing and licking and nipping at my jaw, then my lips, then my neck, until I was dizzy with sensation.

The scratch of his fang against my neck drew a deep sigh from me, followed by a gasp as he delicately pierced my skin. The gentle pull of blood from my vein unraveled pleasure deep in my belly, and I moaned into the bite. His palms slipped down to my shoulders, his fingers splaying across my collarbone and lower, just brushing the tops of my breasts.

Clutching the fabric of his shirt, I pressed my thighs together against the beginning ache.

I moaned again as his fangs slid free of my skin - he was always so careful, and it just made everything so much more sensual. My eyes fluttered open as I felt him place another berry in my mouth, and then he kissed me again. The sweet berry and the dark richness of my own blood mingled as his tongue tangled with mine.

"You're so much everything," he mumbled, and I

held in a giggle. My vampire was a bit drunk, and I fucking loved it.

The blood often affected him like this, and the few times I'd used my horn like a fang, I'd experienced the same delirium. I could see why it might be addictive - and I could see why Jai would never give up his control for anyone but an *aima*. He was completely and forever mine.

His full lips were sliding between my breasts now, pushing the robe out of the way. He bit lightly at my nipple through the violet lace bra I'd put on, and my fingers suddenly came back to life. I scrabbled at his shirt, wishing to see my vampire naked and beautiful in the early morning light.

He allowed the shirt, taking mine in turn. But he stopped me when I reached for his pants.

"Mine," he growled, pushing his hands under my ass and yanking down my matching lace panties. He flicked open the robe, and in an instant, I was the one bare to the growing sunlight. And that was pretty awesome, too.

Jai knelt between my legs, drawing my knees onto his shoulders and scooting my core closer to his tempting mouth. His tongue swiped along my inner thigh, and his fingers pinched the soft skin there, just enough to assert his dominance.

"All yours," I agreed in a whisper as he pushed my hands onto the chair's armrests, warning me in my mind to keep them there.

I let my head fall back on the chair as he began his

assault. My vampire was so in tune with my body that he needed nothing except my stuttering breaths to guide him.

"Jai, yes," I moaned as orgasm rippled through me like waves sucking at the sand. My thighs trembled around his head, but he moved lower, plunging his tongue inside me. His hands pushed my legs wider, and then he reached around to press my lower back into a deep arch, angling my hips down and my breasts up to the sky.

My mouth hung open in a gasp for air as his fingers plunged deep inside me, and I let my eyes slide closed. A shadow passed across my face, but before I could react, another pair of soft lips were pressed to mine, upside down. Dair was standing behind the chair, and he'd taken full advantage of my distraction to lock his hands around my breasts, stealing what was left of my air with his kisses.

My nose was buried in the hollow of his throat, and his rich scent of champagne and tobacco took over my remaining senses, until I was floating - hurtling, really - through a sea of pleasure. The early morning light was swallowed up by his proximity, and I sank into a sultry state of allowing absolutely everything.

JAI

Carlyle's sweet body was writhing under my touch, and it made me feel more powerful than anything I'd ever done with my ice magic. The training in me wanted to stop what I was doing and question Dair immediately, but I squelched that thought easily.

Whatever he'd found about the Oracle could wait a goddamn minute. My beautiful Queen deserved this reprieve, and the treat of both of us pleasuring her as the sun rose over the Champs-Élysées.

Licking a solid line up her slit, I flicked my eyes up to relish the sight of my girl coming apart in ecstasy.

Instead, shock coursed through me as I took in what had to be a glamor. Her skin was as ebony as the night sky, and her hair was flowing around her face like dark water, undulating like she *was* underwater.

But why would she glamor herself now?

As Dair broke away from her kiss and straightened behind her, I glimpsed her slitted eyes, solid black like mine. Like a satisfied cat, she grinned down at me, and I startled again to see a flash of fang.

"Dair?" I whispered, asking him silently if he was seeing this.

The mage cocked an eyebrow at me, stepping around the chair and shaking his head.

"You guys sure know how to run a bed and breakfast," Carlyle murmured, stretching her arms above her head. As I blinked, she appeared normal again, as though the glamor hadn't happened at all.

And maybe it hadn't, if Dair had seen nothing. I shook my head, clearing away all my negative thoughts. Just stress over our current problems, perhaps.

Dair leaned over and fed Carlyle another berry, his thumb catching a runaway bead of ruby juice. I studied her lips, but there was no more sign of fang. Her horn was like a fang, certainly, but I'd never seen her shift into anything with true vampire fangs.

It had to have been a fleeting glamor.

Her cheeks were beautifully flushed, as was the delicate skin on the top of her breasts. Her content and love for us was so evident that it filled my heart near to bursting.

I saw the moment she realized the implication of Dair's return, though, and I cursed the shadow that flitted across her face.

"The Oracle?" she asked, her forehead wrinkling in worry as Dair sank into one of the narrow metal chairs. The look on his face was grim, but he tried to soften it.

"She's alive, though she was indeed attacked. My contact at the Council sent me to the Musée de la Magie, which is where they hid her a few days ago after the attempt on her life. She'll be under their watch for quite some time, but she seemed keen to see you."

"Why would someone try to kill her?" Carlyle asked, her lavender eyes round and worried.

Dair sighed and flicked a tired glance at me. "They

weren't certain, and the Oracle apparently wasn't in the mood to talk. The Council has opened an investigation, of course, but…"

He trailed away, and I glowered. "The timing is just too fucking coincidental," I said, and he nodded.

Carlyle cursed under her breath, and I knew she'd be blaming this on herself too, if we weren't careful.

I felt Dair open his mind to me, giving me an image, and I held in a wince. The Oracle had been attacked, all right. Two broken wrists that may have been self-defense, a thick bandage around her ribs, and a gash across her wrinkled forehead, as though to slice through the third eye *sruth* she possessed. I started to turn away, hoping Carlyle wouldn't see my worry.

"I set an appointment with her, for an hour from now," Dair added.

"So soon," Carlyle muttered to herself. Anxiety flitted across her face, and immediately, Dair and I each had one of her hands in ours.

"No need to worry, Cariño. The Oracle is a friend. She'll have answers for us, I'm certain of it, and she isn't the type to cast blame on us for this mess."

Carlyle nodded, seeming to steel herself. She grabbed her coffee and gulped the rest of it, then stood, the open robe sliding down her back.

"Guess I should get dressed, then."

"It will be a shame, but yes," I murmured, gathering her naked body to me once more. I wanted more - I always wanted more - but we needed to settle this fucking darkblood thing now, before it became a rift in Haret.

I stood and stretched my shirt back over my head, smirking at Carlyle's playful pout. Dair angled between us and snagged her lips for another kiss, and I turned my back to them, staring up at the pale blue sky.

I was doing my best to resist grilling Dair for more intel because I knew he was trying to keep Carlyle calm. The situation was growing more and more worrisome, though.

I didn't understand how children could possibly be tangled up in our future, but I knew one thing for sure. We needed more safety surrounding us before innocents of any kind could be brought into our team's little world.

CHAPTER TEN

CARLYLE

I peered curiously at the bright red storefront Dair had siphoned the three of us to.

"The Oracle is being hidden in a shop?" I asked, cocking my eyebrow at Dair. He grinned.

"The shop is merely a facade. The Counsel has many such hidden places in cities, and the human public is none the wiser because of fine spells and careful glamor."

He knocked smartly on the door, although we were clearly too early for business hours. The street was empty of tourists and I saw only a couple of workers who were just now unlocking their own shops. The magic shop's door opened a sliver, and Dair leaned in to murmur a few words, gesturing back at me.

We were hurried inside by a petite woman in a long black dress, almost something I would have expected for a Halloween witch's costume. She gave me a quick curtsy and muttered something that sounded like "Your Majesty," but her sour expression wasn't exactly welcoming.

Instead, she bustled past the counters where human visitors might buy tickets and brochures, or tacky souvenirs, and ducked under a low stone arch. We hurried after her without a sound, the building looking more and more medieval as we went deeper and the glamor began to fall away.

A spiral stone staircase that reminded me of a fairy-tale tower led us higher than should have been possible, judging from what I'd seen of the outside of the building.

"Thank you," Dair said as we reached the top and paused before a thick, rustic wooden door.

The woman only glared disapprovingly at us, muttering some sort of enchantment that drew bolts apart on the unseen inside of the door. She gave it a shove and waved us on in, not following us. I heard the bolts click shut behind us, one by one.

She's a bit creepy, boss, I whispered in Jai's mind, silently asking him if we needed to be worried about her intentions.

He only shook his head at me, though, and began

checking the perimeter of the room. He slunk along the rough stone wall, and soon his smooth movements were lost in the dark recesses of the enormous round room.

Dair rested his hand on my lower back. "The staff are protective, and for good reason. The Oracle is safe here, though."

After a few quiet minutes, Jai reappeared. He beckoned, and I stepped deeper into the shadows. It took my eyes a few seconds to adjust to the near-darkness around me.

But then I saw her - an ancient-looking fae resting in a low bed with several pillows propping up her frail form, and a light blanket covering her tiny body.

Her eyes shone like two full moons in her sunken face. I knelt next to the woman, noticing her pointed ears in the dim light.

"Come here," she whispered, raising her bandaged hands.

I inched closer. Gently, I placed my hands over hers and met her gaze. Her eyes were eerie, but mesmerizing. I noticed a deep gash in the center of her forehead, glistening with a healing ointment.

"Leave us," she rasped, her eyes sliding back to Dair and Jai. They softened a bit as she looked at my mage. "Thank you for aiding me. My message cannot be hindered now."

Dair bowed his head, and my men retreated to the front of the room.

"You have good mates," she said. I smiled, waiting

a few seconds for her to continue.

"I'm hoping you can tell me about my *sruth*. I was told it's blocked," I started when she didn't. We'd begin with an easy question.

She chuckled and smirked at me. Her breathing was a bit jagged, and her movements were stiff as she turned her head toward me.

"You're here for much more than that. But yes, it is both blocked and strangely mixed. I imagine you can sort that mess out, though, seeing as you mixed it in the first place."

"When I tried to make new Qilin powers?" I asked, and she nodded, wincing at the motion. "Was that a bad thing to do?"

"Just as dark and light are relative, so are good and bad, my young Queen. Each of us is a mix of light and dark, and each of us must sort out our intentions in a given moment to fetch what we truly want from the cosmos."

I blinked at her, uncertain how to tell her I had no fucking clue what she was talking about.

The Oracle rubbed at the wound on her forehead, smearing the medicine a little. "They tried to stop me from seeing, as though that would stop the future from coming." She made a noise of disgust, coughing a little into her sleeve. "The fools don't understand that the future already exists. As soon as you turn your focus on it, it blinks itself into existence. You, girl-queen, already have your answers. You've already solved the riddle and brought the land together.

You've already had your babies. This form here just hasn't caught up with that future form yet." She gestured toward me.

And now I was even more confused, though my intuition and my magic were telling me she was being honest. Her fingers were warm against mine, and I felt the faint pulse of her magic through them. It made my forehead heat, as though I was an ant under the glare of a magnifying glass.

"I don't like the idea that the future is already decided," I blurted, biting my lip. That wasn't anything to do with why I was here.

"Of course, the future is already decided, just as the past is. The only decisions you make now are if you're deciding the future or letting someone else decide it, and which future you'll allow. Futures are an exercise in plurality, you know."

I sighed and slumped against the bed. "I don't know what any of this means," I admitted.

"Oracles aren't known for simplifying things, my dear. We just dump the info on you and then you do the work." She cackled, and the noise made me smile until it ended in a cough.

"So, I *can* have babies, then?" I ventured, since she'd brought up.

"Can and almost certainly will. Oh, they'll be a handful, those two." Her eyes grew faraway, as though she was remembering something - remembering my freaking future, apparently.

"I'm sorry. I just don't even know what to ask. My

sruth is all mixed up, and I don't know how to fix it or why that's even important. And this isn't exactly the time to be bringing babies into the world - not with darkblood rebellions everywhere."

"Babies come into the world when they've agreed to," the Oracle said, her voice sharp. "You did the same, so don't be selfish and try to control them before they're even born."

I knew the tiny old fae was speaking a language I understood, but I was going to need a damn good cup of coffee to figure out what she actually meant.

"Be careful, Qilin," the Oracle said, reaching to grab my hand again. "I don't think the darkbloods mean you harm. But sometimes we do the most harm to ourselves, saving our enemies the trouble."

"Did the darkbloods do this to you?" I couldn't help the question, but she only shrugged.

"I play my role. You have a heartstone, yes?"

I startled at the sudden change of topic. "Yes. The leprechaun - the Herald - left it for me, we think. We found it after he, ah, died."

She nodded, and my cheeks flushed as I wondered if she knew the Herald had died by my horn. "He played his role too, then," she murmured. "Give me that box," she ordered, pointing to a large travel bag a few feet away. I scooted closer and found a black container about the size of a ring box resting on top of some clothing. I handed it to her, but she waved it away.

"You keep that. And if you can't figure out all my

riddles, the Goddess knows them all."

I opened my mouth to ask another question, but the Oracle settled back on her pillow and closed her eyes. It felt like the meeting was over, but just like with Dr. F, I didn't really feel like I'd learned anything.

Still, I wasn't ready to stand and leave, and I didn't sense any restlessness from Dair and Jai. Maybe the Oracle just needed to rest a bit.

Several minutes passed with only her quiet breathing, and I thought she'd fallen asleep. I fiddled with the black box, finally opening it to peek inside.

I had no sooner cracked it open than the Oracle sat straight up in bed, startling me so much the box clattered to the floor.

Her full-moon eyes were huge and nearly glowing, but they weren't focused on me. Her mouth opened, but an entirely different voice spoke the words that came next.

Cover the bruise;
Tighten the noose.
Lightblood carelessly sings;
Darkblood pays the dues.

I gaped at her as she slumped back into the pillows, blinking and yawning like she was just waking up. What the actual fuck was that?

"Oh, sorry, dear. I must have dozed off. Have you gotten what you need?" She tugged the blanket up under her chin.

"The riddle…" My voice trailed off as her eyes glowed again.

"Is everything else I'm supposed to tell you, lightblood. Now run along and solve the mystery, so perhaps I can finally sleep." She smiled at me, but something in the movement of her lips was vicious and animalistic.

I stumbled to my feet, feeling a definite sense that our meeting was over now, and I wouldn't get anything else from her.

According to her, I'd already gotten everything I needed. But goddamn. If the future of Haret depended on me solving this mystery, we were all in a heap of trouble.

Dair met me at the edge of the shadows, and I saw Jai peering out a grimy window.

"I guess I'm ready," I said, fiddling with my fingers. "She basically dismissed me."

Dair glanced at the bed, frowning, but he only shrugged. "More mysteries, Cariño?"

I nodded, pressing my lips together. "Always. We need to have another freaking study session, I guess."

Jai sidled up to me and the two of them led me to the door, where Dair spoke a few words. A chime sounded somewhere beneath us, and I imagined I heard the woman in black clomping up the stairs, though she'd made no noise when we'd arrived.

The door rattled as the bolts and charms were undone, then swung open. She gestured us onto the stairs, and it seemed like barely a breath later and we were back in the shop, staring at a case of movie-prop magic wands in black boxes.

"Oh! I left the box the Oracle gave me!" Realizing I'd never picked it up from the floor after her riddle, I whirled on the old woman, and damn, if looks could kill I wouldn't need to worry about future children.

"Wait here," she hissed, and she was gone before any of us could protest.

"What box, *aima*?" Jai questioned, but I only shrugged.

"I never even got to open it. The Oracle startled me by reciting another freaking riddle, like she was possessed or something. It said, 'Cover the bruise; Tighten-'"

A scream from the tower above us stopped the words in my throat, and Jai shoved past me, racing up the stairs at his vampire speed. Dair and I were left with good old regular speed and aching quads, since the tower was protected from anyone siphoning into it.

Two mages I didn't recognize popped into the shop just as we started up, and they, too, pushed past us, pounding up the stone steps.

"Council Protectors," Dair told me as we hurried.

CHAPTER ELEVEN

CARLYLE

When we arrived and saw the situation, I stumbled back against Dair, feeling my breakfast surging into my throat.

"Impossible," I choked out. We'd only been gone a few minutes.

The Oracle had been strung up from a rafter high in the domed tower, her head hanging at a horrible angle and her face as white as the moon.

"Her attackers somehow returned to finish the job," one of the Council men called, though my brain rejected it.

"We were the only-" I began, but Dair clapped his

hand over my mouth. I slumped against him, realizing with a jolt how this was going to look. "Someone framed us?" I whispered, and Dair hugged me tight.

Suddenly, a snarl and a crash sounded from the far side of the room, and the other Council Protector appeared, dragging another person.

"How did he get in here?" the first Protector yelled, whirling on us. The woman from the shop let loose a stream of caustic-sounding French, pointing wildly at the hissing vampire.

Jai and Dair sprang into action, helping the Protectors contain the mystery man. Still unable to get past the horror of the situation, I flicked my eyes between the men and the woman, who raised her arms and began to recite a spell that brought the Oracle down from the ceiling, placing her body gently back on the bed.

I rushed to kneel next to her, but she was obviously gone. My knee brushed against the box just under the bed, and I hurried to slip it in my pocket before anyone noticed.

"All these bruises" the woman moaned, loosening the black fabric noose from the Oracle's throat. My mind fluttered like a bird in a cage at her words.

"Cover the bruise, tighten the noose," I whispered to myself. Ah, fuck. She'd seen this coming. I glanced at Jai and sent him a quick message that we needed to get the hell out of here.

"Ask the fucking mage," the bound vampire roared at the Protectors, breaking into my thoughts.

"That silk stinks of him and the Queen. Another darkblood death at her majesty's hands," he shouted, just before one of the Protectors held a blade to his throat in warning.

I heard Dair suck in a breath, and a crackle of ice hurtled around the room as my vampire and mage communicated with me. I stared at the fabric that had been wound around the Oracle's neck, refusing to recognize it as the same silk that had bound my own body in bliss only the day before.

Something in my brain screamed in denial, but the evidence was right before me.

Planted evidence, of course, but fucking how?

How did that silk come to be here in this room, and how did it become a weapon? And how so fucking *fast*?

I felt my men behind me, tugging at my hands and leading me step by step backward toward the tower door.

Time to go, aima, Jai ordered in my mind.

"I only came here to warn her…" The other vampire's words ended in a gurgle of blood as the Protector sliced his head away from his neck in one clean move.

"You can't do that," I screamed at him in shock, breaking free of Dair but not Jai. "Fair trial!"

Jai gripped my arm so hard I almost whimpered, again pulling me farther from the bed and the gore of the unfolding execution.

"They can, *aima*. Paris Council has rules for it. We

must go," he repeated, and I felt the hint of his icy magic locking onto my mind.

I knew we had to go, if only for Dair's sake.

If any of them started to look too closely at that black silk, they could surely tie it to my mage. And to me.

"We will be in touch," Dair called as Jai yanked me through the door and nearly pushed me down the first few stairs. "Our majesty is needed in Haret," my mage added, still desperately trying to smooth over our hurried leaving.

I knew it wouldn't help.

People would make of it what they wanted. And what the darkbloods wanted was another death at the hand of their new Queen.

Somehow, it had happened, despite everything I'd vowed.

The second we were on the street, Dair siphoned us back to the hotel room. Jai wrenched the drapes shut and began shoving everything into Dair's travel bag.

I'd never seen him so furious without anyone to unleash it on.

"There was no-one else in that room before," Jai insisted, almost to himself. "He couldn't possibly have done it."

"I'm so sorry, Cariño," Dair murmured. I sank into a chair in shock, and he knelt before me, burying his head in my lap. "It was so foolish of me to bring that silk."

"Shut up, mage," I managed, bending over his dark head and kissing the back of his neck. "It's not like you could have predicted that fuckery."

There was no other word for it. Somehow, the silk had been snitched from Dair and used as an unexpected murder weapon, merely seconds after we'd left the Oracle's room.

We would have been even more obviously framed if that vampire hadn't essentially been caught in the act. Then again, he'd yelled something about a warning just before he…

"Wait," I said, stumbling back over that thought. "Assuming the vampire didn't kill the Oracle, was he there to warn *her* about the threat, or *us* about it?"

Jai snapped his eyes to mine, narrowing them in question.

"This would be a very serious accusation on the Paris Council, then," he replied, jumping another step ahead and putting together their rushed disposal of the would-be murderer. I grimaced.

"That would mean they were covering up for a second group, then. Or themselves," I reasoned. Dair had lifted his head to gaze at me, and I saw the thoughts churning through his mind, too.

"With that silk, they could still frame us for the Oracle - another darkblood murder," he said, and I nodded.

"So, it's possible that whoever the vampire was working with meant to warn us. But he was killed before he could tell the truth. Or maybe he really did kill the Oracle, and the Council acted within their rights." I sighed and pushed Dair away, standing. "I want to go home. No matter how we look at it, another darkblood has died because of me. Two, even, assuming the vampire was darkblood."

Slipping my fingers in my pocket, I checked that the black box was still there.

"What did she give you?" Jai asked, missing nothing.

I drew it out and opened it, frowning when I saw a plain glass marble inside. It was milky, with the glass blown into layers of clear and haze.

"Tell us the riddle," Jai commanded, staring intently at the marble.

"*Cover the bruise; Tighten the noose. Lightblood carelessly sings; Darkblood pays the dues,*" I recited.

Jai cursed under his breath, and I dropped the box as the marble flashed and began to dissolve into sweet-smelling smoke, while a soft ringing tone echoed around us. My vampire darted to catch it before it rolled under the bed, and I backed away as he stared at its new irregular shape.

"A singing stone," Dair murmured. "I've never seen one in person, but it has to be."

"It is," Jai confirmed. He looked up at me. "Carlyle, I'm sorry." He slipped the stone carefully back into the box. I grimaced when he offered it to me, and he tucked it into the bag on the bed.

"Sorry for what?" I asked, my voice tight with anxiety.

"The riddle…I think it framed you as much as anything else. You had to share it with us to get the stone, but in sharing it, the Oracle was destined to die."

I stared at him, trying to absorb his meaning, but all I could understand was that my actions had killed another innocent darkblood.

"I'm a horrible Queen," I said, wrapping my arms around Dair and burying my face in his shirt this time. They both hurried to reassure me, but after that, my men were uncharacteristically quiet as Dair siphoned the three of us back to where the Path waited in the woods, ready to take us home.

I was gathering my energy to carry us over the rainbow when Jai stopped me, dropping a kiss on my forehead.

"Carlyle, I know you blame yourself, but you are a pawn here. We must solve the maze to exit it."

I nodded. Knowing that someone was pulling my strings didn't help at all. "It's just too neat of a coincidence," I said, feeling the sadness finally crack into frustration.

I needed the rest of my men. I may have fallen right into the prophecy by telling Jai and Dair the riddle, but now that it was done, I needed all six of my smart guys helping solve this puzzle.

Dair pressed himself to my back while Jai wrapped his arms around my waist.

"Nothing is truly coincidence, my *aima*," Jai murmured in my ear, sending a thrill crawling down my spine. "Iaga has a plan, and it's up to us to root out the reasons behind the rhymes."

I smiled at his word play, feeling stronger already. Something else he'd said hit me just as I pulled us into the colorful magic. Maybe it was time to find Iaga again and talk to her, instead of running around Haret and Earth.

Maybe it was time to find her where I'd first found her - in a simple stone temple deep in the pride lands of Sol's sunny home.

CHAPTER TWELVE

CARLYLE

The second we were back in the castle, I shocked all my men by giving them an official order to leave me the crap alone. I felt guilty when I saw everyone's faces, but I needed some time to think.

I had to protect them - I had to protect Haret.

If me telling Jai about the riddle had somehow tipped the first domino in the Oracle's death, maybe I needed to reevaluate how much I told my men.

Sitting cross-legged on the bed, I reasoned that I had to be the lightblood - after all, the first riddle had called me the Queen who was more light than dark, and all my previous dealings with Aleron and the Ringmaster had made it obvious too.

Plus, I'd been careless with the information, singing it straight to Jai as soon as he'd asked. I hadn't even checked the area, either - maybe that vampire or someone else had overheard. Maybe even that creepy caretaker woman.

Regardless, the Oracle must be the darkblood who had paid the dues for my carelessness. Just like the Herald fae had paid the dues for my rage.

I may not be an actual darkblood myself, but my darkest qualities certainly were the ones coming out recently.

And so I sat in a huddle in the middle of my massive bed, brain spinning as I held the heartstone in one hand and the singing stone in the other. Just what was I supposed to do with these?

They'd both been presents in a way, and their real natures hadn't been revealed until their owners had died.

I shivered. If *sruth* corresponded to chakra, and assuming I'd need one of each to un-mix my magical energy, then I had five more stones to gather.

Would that mean five more deaths?

By the goddess, I hoped not.

And speaking of the goddess - why exactly would Iaga condone the deaths of her people just to give me a message? Why couldn't she materialize right in front of me like she'd done a dozen times before?

No, I was definitely missing part of the

explanation. Maybe she was even in trouble somehow.

I ached to call my guys in and divulge everything, so they could help me sort it out. But I resisted. I couldn't involve anyone else in this mess. I couldn't risk the possibility that I was supposed to keep this to myself, or more might die.

I held the heartstone up to my chest and closed my eyes, searching within for the swirling green magic that matched the stone's color. Tendrils of it appeared in my imagination, reaching toward the stone, but they weren't long enough. They stretched too thin and dissipated like fog.

Going deeper into my meditative focus, I decided the magic inside me actually did feel muddled, like I'd started with a paint palette of rainbow colors and ended up with muddy water. Dark water.

I realized I'd never even used Paris to explore the darkness in me like I'd suggested to Jai. Unless…maybe it wasn't so much an exploration as a revealing. Two people had already died to send me a message - that alone was pretty damn dark.

With a frustrated sigh, I pushed off the bed and exited the room with a slam of the door.

Maybe I just needed some sugar. I followed my nose to the kitchen, smiling in appreciation when I saw Jai at his finest - shirt off and tossed across his shoulder, cheekbones smudged with flour, and heat from the castle's massive ovens already giving his pale skin a sheen of sweat.

Damn. Who needed sugar with a man like that to look at?

Ah, who was I kidding? I'd take some of both.

"I sent the staff away," Jai said, without even looking up from his measuring. "And the rest of the team is busy grilling Dair and trying to solve the riddle. I told them not to bother us."

"So, you figured I'd find my way down here?" I asked, perching on the huge wooden dining table across the room from him. For now, I was content to watch.

"I figured these smells would help," he answered with a soft smile.

I let several minutes pass by in silence, just appreciating the view. Small things, right? But soon, my melancholy crept back in.

"You know, that wasn't exactly what I'd had in mind when I wanted to explore my darker side," I muttered, knowing Jai would remember my initial plan for Paris. I wrapped my arms around myself. Suddenly, the heat of the room and the warmth of Jai's gaze seemed sucked away, replaced by a bone-chilling cold.

Even when I'd been fighting the Ringmaster and his various nitwit henchmen, I'd always felt like I was at least *trying* to do the right thing.

Now? I had no idea what I was doing, and I feared I was playing right into someone else's plans.

Now, I was pretty much the nitwit henchman.

I couldn't stop shivering, even when heat seared

through the room as Jai pulled a tray of cookies from the oven. It was as if my body had simply started to shut down.

But then my vampire was there, his touch cool but his eyes molten. "None of that was your fault - no matter how you spin it in your mind." He gathered me close and I took in a deep, shuddery breath. I wasn't in the mood to cry. I was in the mood to forget.

Jai had either read my mind or knew me well enough to not need such tricks, because he lifted my chin and kissed my lips gently. One hand stroked along my jaw, guiding the kiss, while the other found my palm and pressed something warm and sticky into it.

I glanced down and giggled, despite myself. A fresh chocolate chip cookie was melting all over my hand.

Jai kissed me once more, then darted back behind the wide island to continue his baking. "I assumed we could use a sweet break," he suggested, and I had to admit I was enjoying the flex of his biceps as he stirred whatever was in the large silver bowl. "Though these macarons will take a while to finish. I might need a sweet break during my sweet break."

I laughed, feeling better already. What had I been thinking, shutting myself away from my men? "How long are we talking?"

"Ah, these will rest on the tray for an hour, then bake for seventeen minutes. Then we have to let them cool a while before filling them. And then there's the overnight resting period before we can eat them."

"All that *and* overnight? Fuck that," I said, laughing even more. "I could take us back to Paris and buy a dozen faster than all that."

He just grinned. "But then we wouldn't have the pleasure of taking the break, would we? Good things are worth waiting for."

I eyed him from across the room, debating whether to pounce and just take him on the kitchen floor, or to wait patiently while he piped the infernal cookies, one at a time, in perfect rows across the baking sheet.

"Hey, baby. Mind if I join you?"

I turned at the soft voice. Damn, I'd missed that sexy dragon. I peered behind him, but he was alone. That was okay, too.

"Thought I'd slip away while they were arguing over where to go next, because I figured you'd already decided," Jack said, his lopsided grinned calling me out in so many ways.

Before I could hop off the table to give him a hug, Jack was crowding between my legs, holding me tight and burying his nose in my neck.

"Goddamn, you smell good," he murmured, the sniff turning into a gentle lick and a less gentle nip that sent a shock of pleasure straight through me.

"That's the macarons," Jai called, but I heard the smile in his voice. I knew they were both trying to distract me, and I decided I would let them. Actually,

I decided I would enjoy the hell out of this distraction.

My knees squeezed against Jack's waist, and his hands slipped down my back, barely giving me warning before he cupped under my ass and pantsed me. My bare ass hit the breakfast table with a smack, and I giggled, wrapping my bare legs around him.

"I know you can toss me on my ass too, if you don't want it," Jack admitted. I only raised an eyebrow before holding my arms in the air like a child waiting to be undressed.

Naturally, Jack obliged.

The click of Jai's wooden spoon against the metal bowl punctuated Jack's nips and sweet kisses down the column of my neck and between my breasts, and I sensed the vampire watching us.

I reveled in it, letting Jack lay me back on the table and spread my knees wide for them both to see. I felt the heat of his mouth long before the actual slick of his tongue, and I was closer to begging that I would have liked.

"Yes, Jack. Please," I whispered as he teased and took his time along my stomach and inner thighs, never actually touching the places I most wanted.

His fingers swept through my folds and pushed inside me, barely a knuckle's length. I moaned in frustration, trying to arch my hips toward him, but he held me fast against the smooth wooden tabletop.

He was without mercy. I sat up and reached forward just enough to rake my fingernails over his chest, and I thought he might cave, but he only stepped back to look at me.

"Fucking gorgeous," he claimed, scanning me from head to bare toes. I grinned as he finally tugged open his belt, giving me a little shimmy of his hips and a body roll that was *my* idea of fucking gorgeous. His hands did exactly what I was hoping, tugging his shirt up so I could watch those abs roll and those slim hips thrust toward me.

"My bachelor party dragon," I teased, as he did a sexy little spin and was on me with nothing more than his boxers. He smirked and picked me right up from the table, settling himself in my place and straddling my legs over his lap. I glanced over my shoulder at Jai, who had finally stopped worrying about the damn cookies.

I made short work of Jack's waistband, moaning as he finally let me sink down on his thick cock. My legs were spread wide enough to pinch and my toes dangled off the table, but his hands clamped around my waist, sliding me up and down his shaft in a smooth, slow rhythm.

My dragon was here for the night.

I let my head fall back, enjoying the brush of my hair against my spine as he kissed leisurely around the fullness of my breasts. A blur of black caught my upside-down attention, and then Jai pushed against my back, his lips pressed tight against my neck.

I gasped into the sensation, begging him for a bite in my mind.

One hand cupped under my chin, keeping my head steady against his chest, but the other tangled in my hair, sliding down my back and the curve of my ass until his fingers squeezed my pussy around Jack's cock. Jack hissed and bit down on my nipple, and I let out an impatient curse.

These men would be the death of me.

Jai's fingers stroked and played back toward my asshole, though, finally breaching that tight place and matching Jack's slow-as-Christmas movements.

"Boss, please," I begged, reaching back to scrape my fingernails along his jaw. I heard him unbuckle his belt, and my body thrilled with the idea of fucking both my mates, in the castle's kitchen of all places. Just as I was struggling to get some traction with my toes, Jai stepped back and knotted my hair up with one of his elastics.

The cool rim of a glass jar pressed against my neck, and I looked down to see a golden trail of lavender honey sliding down my chest, right between my aching breasts.

Jai and Jack went for the sweetness at the same time, and my back arched into a crescent moon as Jai's fangs broke my skin, my blood mingling with the sticky-sweetness of the honey.

He moaned into the taste, his mind wide open for me to experience. Jack's tongue was lapping up the rest, then sucking at my nipple. Jai drank for several long, breathless minutes, his fingers driving me closer to insanity as he toyed with my asshole, stroking across and around, before stretching me gently.

As his fangs pulled free of my skin, his cock nudged against my opening, and I leaned into Jack, kissing him fiercely as Jai's cock slid deep inside me. I was pinned from back to front, caught in a sticky trap of wonder.

The two of them moved like one person, rocking me on gentle waves of near oblivion.

I felt my mind sort of leaving my body with the intensity, feeling like I was in another dimension of pleasure. I could almost imagine looking down at myself with my two mates.

My first mate, and my last. The fire of my dragon mingled with the ice of my vampire. Polar opposites in so many ways, though I couldn't exactly say one was light and one was dark - they were both a mix of the two.

And there was my answer.

I wasn't one or the other, either.

Suddenly the riddle we'd been given in Aralia came to mind, and I jolted back into the moment. Our bodies were rocking faster now, each of us chasing the other in a circle of mind-bending bliss. Orgasm rippled through me first, and my men came quickly after, as though they'd been just waiting for me to tip over the edge.

We tumbled to the tabletop in a sticky, heaving, sated mess, and I grinned up at the ceiling.

"Nothing like a little sugar to clear the mind," I murmured, my breath still coming in short gasps.

"And what did you find in your clarity, baby?" Jack asked, propping his arm behind his head and playing with the honey on his chest.

"Dragon's fang and vampire's wing," I said, gesturing to both of them. Of course, I got puzzled stares. I shrugged, leaning my head against Jai's collarbone. It was just the edge of an idea, really. "My magic is mixed up, like the riddle is mixed up. Like a baby is a mix of its parents. I'm not sure how it's all connected, but the Oracle said I already had children, in the future. She said they were a handful," I added, and Jai chuckled.

"Any child of yours certainly would be," he agreed.

"Or child of *yours*," I shot back. "So, if all this is mixed up, maybe that's not the problem. Because the one thing that's *not* mixed up is my light and dark. I'm always trying to keep it separate. But you're both. I'm both. We're all a bit of both."

Jack made a noise of agreement, but I wondered if Jai was really following what I was saying. I didn't have all the pieces yet, but intuition was telling me I was on the right track.

"I want to go visit Iaga - in the temple where I first met her. Field trip to the pride lands?" I suggested, and Jai slipped his arm under my shoulders, hugging me tight.

"It's still risky, traveling in Haret now," he said, his voice gravely.

"It's risky *not* traveling now," I reminded him. "We need some guidance - from someone who can't die,"

I added, my chest tightening. "But I'm done worrying about making the right choice. I'm going to trust the Oracle and *make* a choice. I don't want fear to take that choice from me. I want to live my life from a place of love. Fuck fear."

Jack leaned up to plant a sloppy kiss on my mouth, and I tasted the violet honey on his lips. Jai met my neck again, licking gently at the already-healed place where he'd bitten before. I relaxed into the sweetness that was my mates, and the knowledge and certainty that was mine, if I began to trust myself more.

The future I wanted already existed, according to the Oracle. I just had to give it my attention, and it would blink into existence. I'd figure out what that meant as I moved forward, because I'd be damned if I was going to sit back and let someone else decide this life for me.

WANT MORE?

This mystery continues soon in the next installment of *Sugar Bites* – a set of novellas chronicling the shenanigans Carlyle and her men get up to in their happily-ever-after.

Keep up-to-date and find Laurel and the Piece of Qilin fans in the Facebook reader group
LOVERS OF HARET.
https://www.facebook.com/groups/676410892715276/

Join Laurel's newsletter for new release information, sales, and special, sexy bonus content.
https://laurelchaseauthor.com/newsletter/

REVIEWS

Please consider leaving an honest review on your favorite reading and retail sites.
Lots of readers depend on reviews and recommendations to find their next read.

Love, Laurel

LaurelChaseAuthor.com

AUTHOR'S LOVE NOTE

Dear Reader,

I want to thank you first and forever – you are the best thing about this business, and the reason this novella series exists.

If it weren't for your encouraging comments in our Lovers of Haret group and your amazing reviews, I would never have thought to continue Carlyle's story past the initial series.

Thanks so much for hanging out in the Lovers group and for encouraging me through some hard times. I wish this book had been out sooner, but I'm so grateful for readers who wait!

All my love to the dream team. Alisha keeps me on track socially, while my editor, my cover designer (Christian Bentulan), my betas (Cecily, Alisha, Leanne, and Laura), and my ARC team, all work so hard to make these books way better than I could on my own.

And of course, my family – thanks for always finding the unicorn in the moment. ;)

Stay sexy and sweet, Lovers!

See you next book!

Love, Laurel

ABOUT THE AUTHOR

Laurel Chase lives in the state that boasts of fast
horses, fast cars, and fast women.
She writes steamy romance and lives in her head more
and more each day – hey, the scenery is great in there.
She never sleeps enough, and she drinks too much
coffee, but she'd never replace any of that with
sensible stuff.

Find her hanging out on social media,
usually in the Lovers of Haret readers' group!

www.ingramcontent.com/pod-product-compliance
Lightning Source LLC
Chambersburg PA
CBHW072236150726
48002CB00005B/2119